A LOSS OF
PATIENTS

A LOSS OF PATIENTS

by
Ralph McInerny

A
FATHER DOWLING
Mystery

THE VANGUARD PRESS
NEW YORK

Designer: Tom Torre Bevans
Manufactured in the United States of America.
1 2 3 4 5 6 7 8 9 0

Library of Congress Cataloging in Publication Data

McInerny, Ralph M.
    A loss of patients.

    I. Title
PS3563.A31166L6   1982   813'.54   82-8572
ISBN 0-8149-0826-8   AACR2

For Pat and Ron Weber

A LOSS OF
PATIENTS

1

THE ANCIENT elms and maples which, with the church and rectory of St. Hilary's, had survived the westward expansion that had engulfed Fox River, Illinois, released the golden coin of autumn. Marie Murkin, kerchief tied over her head, sweater buttoned, surveyed the fallen and falling leaves with a grim expression. Her grip tightened on the broom she held.

"Are you landing or taking off, Marie?"

The housekeeper turned to face the smiling Captain Keegan, who stood in the doorway of her kitchen.

"Instead of making jokes, you might be out there helping Father Dowling clean up those leaves."

"I wondered where he was."

Marie humphed. "Wondered? The whole world can see the man out there asking for a heart attack while his parishioners sit on their hands." Phil Keegan came out on the back porch and stood beside the housekeeper. The pastor of St. Hilary's stood encircled by the leaves he had been pulling toward himself with a fan-shaped bamboo broom. He was not the disconsolate figure Marie Murkin's tone suggested. At the moment his head was thrown back as if to welcome the leaves that drifted down from the maple trees above. Phil Keegan left the porch and crossed the lawn to his old friend. The crisp complaint of the leaves as he waded through them brought back memories of childhood. The pleased expression on Roger Dowling's face made it clear that he did not regard his task as penitential. "Need any help, Roger?"

"Not really. But if you could pry that broom from Marie, I'd appreciate it. She's dying to help and I'd much rather she didn't. She has better things to do than rake leaves."

Phil Keegan looked at the priest. He had known Dowling when they were both boys, students at Quigley, the preparatory seminary of the Chicago Archdiocese. Keegan, whose mind refused to accommodate the intricacies of Latin, served in the Army as an MP, came home to marry and father two daughters, as well as advance in his career in the Fox River Police, rising to his present post as chief of detectives. Keegan had been overjoyed when his old friend was assigned to this parish west of Chicago. They became closer friends than they had been in their youth. Keegan, eager for justice; Dowling, mediator of a mercy he himself had needed. Perhaps it was inevitable that Dowling should be a Cub fan. The fact that Phil Keegan too was a faithful follower of the hapless northside nine suggested that there was room for more than law and order in his heart.

"We mustn't keep Marie Murkin from her important tasks," Phil said with heavy irony. He returned to where Marie Murkin, holding her broom with both hands, awaited him. "Come fly with me," he crooned in a painfully inept imitation of Frank Sinatra. Marie hurled the broom at him. She had never cared for the singer and was annoyed at the thought that, after a dissolute life, he had made his peace with the Lord.

"Go help Father," she said, turning on her heel and going into her kitchen.

Phil Keegan returned across the yard to Roger Dowling. The crisp sound of the leaves seemed mournful now. For half an hour the two men worked steadily, filling several large plastic bags with leaves. They emptied them in the street beside the curb. Keegan touched a match to the pile and a thin wisp of white smoke arose, then a tongue of flame, and finally, the delicious smell of burning leaves. The moment seemed the purpose of their effort. The two exchanged a look, no longer men at the half-century mark. The sound of the kitchen door slamming and of Marie Murkin's scream arrived simultaneously. The housekeeper came flying toward them across the lawn, a look of near panic on her face.

"Stop! You can't *do* that. Burning leaves is against the law!"

"Not this week, Marie. The mayor authorized leaf-burning for a ten-day period. Relax."

The housekeeper looked at him skeptically. But her eyes drifted toward the burning leaves and again her expression was one of panic.

"It's all right, Marie," Father Dowling said. "We'll be careful."

She stared at the pastor, momentarily angry; then, hands plunged into the pockets of her sweater, went scuffling back into the house.

"What's that all about, Roger?"

"She had a bit of a scare and it has made her very nervous."

Dreaming of a fire engulfing the rectory, Marie Murkin had wakened to look at the red glow of the vigil light she kept burning before a statue of St. Anthony of Padua. Half asleep, half awake, she had leaped from her bed and come thundering down her stairs to the kitchen. The rapidity of her descent would have been the envy of a fireman. She continued into the yard and it was there that Father Dowling managed to convince her that the house was not on fire.

Marie was only slightly embarrassed. God sends His warnings in dreams. Father Dowling found church-goods catalogs on his desk opened to the display of electric vigil lights. He found the throwing of a switch a repellent stand-in for prayer. The housekeeper was not amused when he suggested he might turn in his pipe for an electric one.

"Women," Phil Keegan muttered good-naturedly, shaking his head.

"Maybe she's right," Roger Dowling said, but Phil was not to be teased.

"What do you think of Barbara Rooney, Roger?"

"Tell me about her."

Phil began the story as they walked to the house and continued it through dinner and when they settled down in the pastor's study.

The body of Barbara Rooney, a woman of thirty-four, had been found in the bathroom of the Rooney home a week before. The cause of death had been loss of blood. The body lay in a mixture of lukewarm water and her own blood, which had flowed from her slashed wrists. There was a suicide note in the carriage of the portable typewriter in Mrs. Rooney's room. The message was not brief but Phil Keegan did not need to refer to any notes in order to convey it to Roger Dowling.

DEAR FRANK: THEY SAY THIS IS THE COWARD'S WAY. I HOPE THEY'RE RIGHT. SORRY FOR THE MESS. THIS ONE AND THE OTHERS. SORRY I'M NOT SORRIER. IF YOU DON'T WANT TO KEEP JASPER I'LL UNDERSTAND. WATER THE PLANTS. B.

Roger Dowling wanted it repeated so that he could write it down. Phil Keegan obliged, and when the priest had it and was pondering it, puffing on his pipe, Keegan waited. "Is it in character, Phil?"

"You knew her as well as I did, Roger."

"Then you didn't know her at all. I spoke with her once, on the telephone. They had been registered in the parish and I wanted to learn why I never saw them. She didn't want to talk about it and that was that. But you have sources other than personal experience on which to base an assessment of this note."

"It doesn't matter. She didn't write it."

"Oh?"

"The note was in her typewriter, but that wasn't the machine on which it had been typed. There was another machine downstairs in the study. Her husband's. The note was written on that machine."

"By whom?"

"The keyboard of the typewriter in the den had been wiped clean. And something else, stranger still. There was no razor in the bathroom except an electric one. Nothing she could cut her wrists with."

"So you don't know whether it was a suicide or murder or an accident?"

"An accident!"

"The circumstances are odd enough to permit the oddest explanations, aren't they? Or is there more? You haven't arrested anyone, have you?"

"For what? Typing a phony letter?"

"You think it's phony?"

"It is unless Barbara Rooney typed it downstairs, wiped the keyboard clean, took it upstairs, and stuck it in the carriage of her own machine. While she was at it she could run a tub of water, slash her wrists, get rid of the razor, and then get into the tub and die."

Phil Keegan was ashamed of the anger and discouragement in his voice. He sounded as if he thought it was Roger's fault they had this weird problem. If they even had it.

"What do you mean, Phil?"

† 5 †

"Robertson would like Phelps to write it off as a suicide. This would take Rooney off any possible hook, and, given Rooney's importance downtown, Robertson thinks that would be great."

"What's stopping him?"

"Not the coroner. Phelps would be perfectly content to call it suicide. No, it's Rooney. He won't hear of it. He insists his wife would never kill herself."

"Meaning that he is innocent or very shrewd."

Keegan gave Dowling everything they knew, which wasn't much, and they mulled it over without result. Well, he hadn't expected the facts to look different just because he laid them out to Father Dowling. No, that wasn't true. He had hoped for something. Many times such exchanges in the study of St. Hilary's parish house had opened up a new angle of vision. But not tonight. When they came in from the bonfire, they had washed and then sat down to a splendid dinner Marie Murkin had waiting for them. Father Dowling assured the nervous housekeeper there was no danger from the fire that still smoldered at the curb. When they left the table, they had gone out and covered the fire with its own ashes. Then, for nearly three hours they had sat in Roger Dowling's study, the priest sipping coffee and relighting his pipe, Phil chewing on a cigar and drinking beer. The evening was worthwhile for the companionship alone. To hell with the Rooney case.

It was nearly eleven when Phil Keegan went out to his car. As always, he was reluctant to leave the rectory and face the drive back to his lonely apartment. He hated the apartment. His balcony overlooked a pond on which pampered ducks floated, though fifty yards beyond was the Fox River. His wife was dead, his two daughters grown and living far off in opposite directions. He found it difficult not to think that the three of them had deserted him.

Sometimes he entertained the fantasy that he had remained in the seminary, become a priest, and thus was eligible to move into the rectory with Roger. This was ridiculous. A fine priest he would make, grumbling at all the changes that had taken place in the Church. Thank God Roger Dowling had not flipped like so many other priests. Phil Keegan could always count on hearing a valid Mass at St. Hilary's.

Arrived at his car, he stopped and looked back at the rectory and the church beyond. The light was on in Roger's study and there was a faint glow from the window of Marie Murkin's room. There was still the aroma of burning leaves. Theirs had not been the only bonfire in the neighborhood. Phil walked down the curb and stirred the ashes with the toe of his shoe. No embers, only ashes. Remember, man, that you are dust and into dust you shall return. Ash Wednesday. It was difficult to think of the dead body of Barbara Rooney in terms of dust. Dust and fire. Phil Keegan made a disgusted sound and went back to his car. It was time to go home to his empty apartment and to the spoiled ducks outside his window.

2

AT THE age of forty-two, Martin Olson had achieved far more than he had dreamed would be his only fifteen years out of dental school. His financial goals had not envisaged the crazy effects of inflation, either on his fees or on the return he would get on his money. "Capital," his father had told him. "Capital. Only money that is the fruit of other money carries the note of wealth." His father's advice, while sound, had not been founded on positive experience. Olson senior had died intestate. Intestate. What a word. To Martin it suggested that his father had been emasculated. He had certainly been broke. There was no insurance at all, not even a burial policy. When he consigned his father to the earth, Martin felt he was closing a bad account. But his father's incantatory advice about capital had stuck deep in Martin's psyche. He resolved to live and die otherwise than his father had.

As a freshman in high school, Martin spent hours of careful study with his counselor, surveying prospective careers. The counselor thought Martin was precocious. But soon it became clear that Martin meant business. He wanted accurate data on salaries, on years of study or other preparation necessary. When he settled on dentistry, his decision was calculated to the finest decimal point. He made a list of pros and cons. The chief drawback was the time it would take him to get his D.D.S. Many years, expensive years, lay between him and his goal. He would be in debt when he finished dental school and he would immediately go deeper into debt in order to set himself up in practice. Not that loans would be hard to come by. It would be an unimaginative banker indeed who was not eager to lend money to a professional man. It was money in the bank, so to speak.

On the plus side, first of all, was the mean income of dentists in the Midwest. Martin had no intention of leaving his native Illinois. As a resident of the state, his prospects of being admitted to dental school at the University of Illinois were better and the tuition would be less for him than for an out-of-stater — an advantage that would not only be lost if he went elsewhere but would be transformed into a grievous disadvantage: as a nonresident he would pay through the nose. And he would make contacts at Illinois that would serve him well in the future — if he and his contacts were neighbors, that is. He would go off to dental school from Fox River and he would return to Fox River to set up his office.

And so it turned out, with the modification that Martin became a specialist in oral surgery. Martin Olson, D.D.S. prospered. The building that housed his offices belonged to him. He was its only resident. He owned another building in which he rented space to five doctors and dentists. To his father's advice, Martin would add property. Capital and property: here was the two-lane highway to financial independence — indeed to affluence. Alas, Martin had no son to whom he might give this advice.

He had never married. Until he was in his mid-thirties,

he did not regret this. To the degree this was possible, he seemed not even to notice it. He was exclusively preoccupied with achieving his financial goals. Not that Martin was a monk. He had his little flings, there had been indiscretions in Las Vegas and in Acapulco. But the girls involved had been no more permanent than the impersonal hotel room he occupied. He felt neither regret nor remorse when he boarded the plane for the return flight to O'Hare.

But, when he was thirty-seven, it occurred to him that a wife and family represented not only an outlay of money, constant demands of cash—there was something else as well. At the Fox River Country Club he became aware of the oddity he was. Other men golfed with their sons and played tennis with their daughters. At club dances they showed up proudly displaying their wives. Martin could find golf and tennis partners easily enough, but dances and dinners were another thing. Nor was a date the solution. The dress a date wore did not symbolize the success of Martin Olson; her jewelry was not a visible sign of Martin Olson's affluence. And that was not all. Other men had a woman in whom to confide, a partner who could be entrusted with full knowledge of how well they were doing and praise them for it. His accountant and broker were no substitute for this.

Martin began to see his women patients in a new way. His staff numbered eleven, all of them female, but they did not interest him. If they were not too old or unattractive, they seemed far too distant from the well-groomed sophistication of the wives of his fellow members of the Fox River Country Club. Some of these wives were his patients. He came to know the meaning of the term "covet" as used in the Decalogue. He cast a speculative eye on other men's wives and if he ranked them, inevitably, as much on the condition of their teeth as on their external appearance, it was remarkable how the two coincided.

Barbara Rooney's dental chart affected him as dirty books do other men and her x-rays had an erotic effect on Martin that could not have been rivaled by less equivocally pornographic film. There was a little recession of her gums, but thank God for that. It was what brought her to him for the minor surgery that would put an end to the remote risk of pyorrhea she ran. The patter he had developed to divert his patients while he operated drew an unexpected reaction from Barbara Rooney.

What Martin did while the patient was under local anaesthetic, mouth full as it must seem of hands and instruments and blood, was to carry on a little guessing game with his technical assistant. Is he/she married? How many children? What work or hobby does she/he have? Inane, silly, but it made the time pass.

"What a damned silly thing to do when a person is defenseless. I tried to bite your hand, do you know that? How I wanted to tell you to shut up."

Barbara Rooney said all this with a frowning smile, sitting on the edge of a chair on the other side of his desk, leaning toward him. If this was an insult, it rang in his ears like a siren song.

"I'm sorry. I didn't mean to offend you. But you're the first one who's ever complained."

"I don't believe it."

"It's true."

Her hair, he decided, was honey blonde. She wore green eye shadow and pale lipstick and the flesh of her oval-shaped face was smooth and tanned. He told her that he would like to see her every month for a checkup.

"Every month?"

"It's just routine."

She accepted this but of course Wanda Wippel, his senior staff person, was surprised at the frequency of Mrs. Rooney's visits.

"It reassures her," Martin Olson said, thereby taking the first fatal step "when first he practised to deceive." Checkups were left to assistants as a rule, Dr. Olson being called in for the merest glance at the end of a session, called in from other labors to pass definitively on a patient's progress. But he was unwilling to entrust Barbara Rooney to anyone else. "I promised her husband," he whispered to Miss Wippel, rolling his eyes in resignation. Her wonderment — it would be too much to call it suspicion — turned to sympathy. How simple it all was.

Frank Rooney, the allegedly concerned spouse, was the merest of acquaintances at the time. Martin Olson decided to cultivate Rooney. This was not an easy thing to do. Frank Rooney was enormously wealthy, but his money did not represent a personal achievement. He had been born rich. He had been raised rich. He had even married rich. His law degree had been attained almost inadvertently. Within a year of passing the bar exams he was a member of his father's firm. The more Martin Olson learned of Frank Rooney, the less he liked him. Jealousy is a powerful stimulus. Martin Olson, who had been flirting with complacency, renewed his acquisitive efforts, expanded his practice, built another building, invested with somewhat more daring, the better to increase his worth. Within two years he doubled his capital and he had the odd thought that he was doing this for Barbara Rooney, or to spite Frank Rooney, or both. For those two years his passion for Barbara Rooney remained a matter of fantasy and imagination. It entered the real world in a classically accidental fashion. He and Barbara Rooney met in the shelter off the twelfth tee as in a rendezvous one rainy afternoon in late July.

The meeting was accidental only for Barbara Rooney, not for Martin. He had been a student of her movements for some time and her habit of playing the back nine on Thursday afternoons had of course come to his attention. Up to that time Wednesdays had always been his weekly day off.

Thursday was a completely untypical day at the Fox River Country Club. Deserted fairways stretched before the beholder as he stood on the clubhouse porch. Martin watched Barbara drive from the tenth tee and then go off, a solitary figure in her cart, under

the threatening skies. He had meant to catch up with her and propose that they continue together. What could be more natural? In
the event, the heavens opened, the rains came, and he rushed into
the shelter to find his quarry waiting for him.

"This is a dumb day to be golfing," she said, seemingly
unsurprised by his sudden appearance.

"I feel the same way."

"I meant you, not me. If I'm interrupted today, I can golf
tomorrow. Your weekly chance is gone." She paused and looked at
him. Her golf skirt displayed her sinewy yet shapely legs, the great
bill of her golf cap put her face intriguingly in shadow. Her ponytail
was damp with rain but retained a saucy bounce. "I thought you
golfed on Wednesdays. All doctors golf on Wednesdays."

"I golf when I like."

This phony bravura seemed to make her more interested
in him than she had been before. Did she see him as a nonconformist,
a man who walked to his own music? This image of himself appealed
to Martin Olson. It was to be the persona he developed for Barbara
Rooney. That Thursday afternoon, in the shelter, with rain pelting
on the roof at first and then subsiding to sad dripping from the eaves,
Martin Olson resolved that Barbara Rooney would be his.

This doomed hope required that he regard her marriage
to Rooney as a bagatelle, her two little boys of trivial moment. Even
more unrealistically, it required the hope that Barbara Rooney would
love him and love him sufficiently to leave all to be at his side. It
emerged that her reluctance to do this had little to do with attach-
ment to her husband or children. But of course he did not know this
at first. At first he was simply crushed by the realization that she
found him a comic figure, of interest only as a source of mild amuse-
ment. The intimacy involved in working on her teeth did not transfer
to the golf course, to the shelter in which they sat with rain dripping
from the eaves, puddles forming in the gravel outside, the pennant
on the flag of the twelfth hole limp and sodden, a symbol of defeat.

But Martin Olson refused to accept defeat. He had attained every goal he set for himself. Besides, his father had been lucky in love if nothing else. If two marriages and a succession of shabby liaisons could be called luck. Martin Olson smiled back at Barbara Rooney, a good loser determined to win.

3

THE PARISH of St. Hilary in Fox River was not high on the list of any cleric who wanted to think of his career in terms of a rising line, each assignment an improvement over the previous one. The fact was that it would not have appeared on such a list at all. It was not so much an assignment as exile. Oh, there had been a time when it was a lively parish, when the school had teemed with eight grades of kids, the church had been packed for six Masses on Sunday, and the street that ran in front of the church, cordoned off for two blocks, had been the scene of a parish bazaar that was the talk of Chicago.

But all that had been long ago, back in the days when many things were different. When several Chicago teams had been contenders, when... Roger Dowling smiled the thought away. He was not tempted by nostalgia. In what had been the good old days of the parish, he had been on the upper rungs of the clerical ladder of success, an important member of the Archdiocesan Marriage Court. His doctorate in canon law, his work on the court, put him in the small group from which the bishops of the future are chosen.

He had been saved from success by failure, by drink. He drank because of the sad parade of broken lives that marched through his days, broken lives no court could mend; and the ecclesiastical court could not even give them the relief they were sure would make a difference. So Roger Dowling had begun to drink and the alcohol he consumed eventually consumed him. He ended in a sanatarium that catered to clerics, off in the fastness of Wisconsin. It took him a while to realize that God had done him a favor. Even when he first came to St. Hilary he had accepted what he imagined would be the average priest's judgment of a parish choked by the highways and interstates that had enclosed it in a triangle, surrounded it with noise, destroyed property values, sent couples with families to raise fleeing westward to more serene suburbs. The Bermuda Triangle, Phil Keegan called it. Phil did not live in the triangle himself, not really. His condominium on the river was north of the parish.

It was three days after Phil had stopped by and helped him rake that Francis X. Rooney came by to see the pastor of St. Hilary. Roger Dowling was uncharacteristically in the front parlor when the car drove up to the curb. He passed Marie Murkin in the hallway.

"I'll be in the study, Marie."

She sailed on, her martyr's sigh drifting in her wake. Marie felt that the clutter of the study was a reflection on her diligence as a housekeeper. The room was out of bounds to her cleaning zeal. Perhaps because it was lined with bookshelves, the study was a better place for conversations that might become confidential. The parlor had its uses, but Roger Dowling found it an impersonal antiseptic place. He preferred to have people see him in his natural surroundings.

"Now don't blame this mess on me," Marie Murkin said a moment later, ushering the visitor into the room. "He won't let me give this room the cleaning it needs." She turned and huffed back to the kitchen as if washing her hands of the whole affair.

"My name is Frank Rooney, Father." He extended his

hand tentatively and Father Dowling took it. Rooney was a tall man, narrow-shouldered, prematurely gray, with a face that was either youthful or weak. His eyes had the expression of one who had recently suffered a painful shock unfamiliar in its magnitude. Rooney did not look like a man who had felt many of life's slings and arrows. Father Dowling put him in the chair favored by Phil Keegan. If Rooney even noticed the room he was in he gave no sign of it.

"You tried to contact us once, Father."

"Yes, I remember."

"You had every right to. My family always belonged to Saint Hilary. What's left of it."

"Has it changed much?"

"I meant the area. All the highways roaring through here. But we kept the house, Barbara and I. You know what happened to Barbara, don't you?" Rooney asked the question as if it were inconceivable that anyone could be unaware of his tragedy.

"I've read what was in the paper."

"The implication was there. Father, she did not commit suicide. Anyone who knew Barbara knows she would never have ended her own life."

"Is that on her death certificate, that she killed herself?"

"That's what they want to put there. Then they can file Barbara away and not have to find the one responsible for her death."

"Then you think she was murdered?"

"Of course she was murdered. I'm sorry, Father. I don't mean to sound insulting. But since she did not kill herself and it certainly could not have been an accident, it must be murder."

"Those do seem to exhaust the possibilities. Wasn't there a note?"

"Yes. It doesn't matter." His voice sounded as if he genuinely thought the note did not matter. "The fact that they did not find the razor used to slash her wrists is far more significant. The killer must have taken it away with him. The police have searched the neighborhood in vain. Anybody can type a note."

"On your typewriter?"

For the first time, Rooney seemed completely in the room. He stared at Father Dowling. "That wasn't in the paper."

"It's true, isn't it?"

"Who told you that?"

"Does it matter?"

"How much more do you know? I don't want to waste time telling you what someone else already has."

"Who is Jasper?"

Rooney's eyes widened slightly, a minimum concession to surprise. "Barbara's dog. So you know what the note said."

"The murderer must have known the name of her dog."

"The beast had a name tag."

"Had?"

"It was put to sleep. I could never stand the dog. That's the point of the mention."

"That makes it sound as if your wife wrote the note."

"Of course it does. We are dealing with an extremely cunning killer."

Could Rooney mean himself?

"Who would want to kill her?"

Rooney looked across at him. His face retained a slightly pained and puzzled look. His main grief appeared to be that this had happened to him. "I wish now you had had a chance to speak with her, Father."

"I did speak with her."

"I mean a real talk."

"About the faith?"

"We should have been Catholics. I guess we were, in a way. Perhaps one never really leaves the Church. That's why you wanted to talk with us, wasn't it?"

"Why did you stop practicing your religion? Or were you attending Mass somewhere else?"

Rooney shook his head. "No. Why did we stop? It's easier to say when. When everything began to fall apart."

"How do you mean?"

"The changes. Dropping Latin, all the rest of it. Things that were once forbidden became okay. It didn't make a lot of sense. And some priest told Barbara it didn't really matter whether a person was Catholic or not. We just stopped attending Mass."

"Well, you weren't the only ones. Is this what you came to talk about?"

"More or less. Do you mind if I smoke?"

"When I'm smoking a pipe?"

"Many people object to cigarettes."

"Go ahead."

Rooney smoked like a boy sneaking a forbidden pleasure. He cupped the cigarette in his hand and kept his hand out of sight for the most part. He said, "Barbara hated it that I couldn't quit smoking. Neither could she."

"How do you mean, more or less?"

"I'm worried about Barbara. About the way I buried her. There was no funeral, just a sort of nondescript thing at the funeral home before the burial. I want you to bless her grave. It was stupid not to think of that before. You can see what it must look like. If a priest wouldn't bury her, there must have been something wrong in the way she died. That's what people will think. If you come bless the grave, well..."

"Is that all a blessing means to you? A guard against malicious gossip?" Roger Dowling spoke softly, meaning to chide Rooney but not wanting to hurt his feelings.

Rooney looked at Roger Dowling but only gradually grasped what was being implied. "Can't a blessing serve several purposes?"

4

No ONE at the Fox River Country Club thought of Georgie Linger as a man in the neighborhood of forty. Few ever thought of his family name, for that matter. He was just Georgie, as he had been for a quarter of a century to the members, their wives, their children. He began working at the club as a caddy, when there still were caddies, not electric carts, so that was one clue to his longevity. Older members had seen his familiar face — gap-toothed smile, carrot-red hair, drooping left eyelid, the merest suggestion as he walked of the limp that had kept him out of the service, kept him young — but they were as unaware of him as they were of the clubhouse itself when first glimpsed as one came in from the county road, twisting among huge oaks and then sweeping around the tennis courts and pool. Who takes real notice of the sky or sun? Unless of course the weather becomes a matter of interest as, during the golf season, it always is.

From caddying Georgie had moved inside to the pro shop where he cleaned clubs after a round, made sure a member's bag was waiting for him on the tee at the start of a scheduled round, looked after things in the shop when Stan Grainger was out giving a lesson or holed up in his hideaway, a storage room beyond the locker area, drinking and grumbling about the sons of bitches to whose pampered wishes he must cater. Grainger was plagued by democratic bias in a plutocratic stronghold. His anguish might have been assuaged if he had been able to join the enemy, but several attempts to make it on the P.G.A. tour had ended ignominiously. The game Grainger could play with such skill alone, with friends, or with a client, deserted him when he teed up among his supposed peers. He was no good in competition and, for a golfer, that is like a doctor's being a good diagnostician except when confronted by an ailing person.

Grainger had turned an old storage room into a little pocket of peace where he could review his grievances and drink. Georgie claimed the room after the scandal that ended Grainger's employment at the club. The pro had been salty with members when he gave them lessons, laying out the weaknesses of their game with a wounding directness. But the correctives he prescribed were invariably helpful, so much was forgiven him. But not when he reeled from his hide-out into the locker room and began berating the be-toweled members, the club, their wives, and the general drift of Western civilization.

Fairwell, the new pro, did not drink, golfed like a dream, preferred outdoors to in, and left Grainger's old hide-out as well as the pro shop in Georgie's hands. He even got him a small raise. This was more than welcome, although Georgie had long been supplementing his income by levying an unknown tax on the members. He had access to all lockers and the wallets therein. He never took more than a dollar from any wallet at a given time. It added up over the course of a season—several hundred dollars a month. Not much, but why be greedy? Georgie was into the money market before most people heard about it, but he kept his ears open in his hide-out behind the locker rooms. Over the years he had fixed it up, making it more comfortable than it had been under Grainger. There was a desk and swivel chair, a cork board on the wall, and an easy chair that reclined like a dentist's chair.

That had been Dr. Olson's observation when he peeked in on Georgie one day. Georgie hadn't liked that. He didn't want his privacy disturbed by members, particularly not by Olson, who was an oddball to begin with. The whole point of the back room was that it be a hideaway. Olson's appearance in his doorway unannounced had damped Georgie's big plan. Why not put a bed in the hideaway and move in? A hideaway bed, that's what they were called. Think of the money he would save if he could sleep right there at the club.

Not that Georgie wanted to change jobs, become the caretaker. Nothing like that. Oh, he had thought of it and he might have gotten the job when Jenkins got it. The caretaker had always been a family man and Jenkins was that. Fay Jenkins weighed three hundred pounds. That had worked against Jenkins, who had been on the grounds crew since the fifties. But the committee had been unable to find a legally acceptable way of saying they couldn't hire Jenkins because his fat-ass wife was an eyesore. Georgie had heard it all from the locker room.

With Barlew, who had done maintenance at the club briefly, Georgie had installed the one-way mirror on the locker room wall. This gave him a good view of the area outside his hideaway though most of the time he kept the drape pulled over it. Who wants to watch a bunch of middle-aged men running around nude? Barlew wanted them to install such a vantage point on the women's locker room but Georgie nixed that. He knew now that he was at the Fox River Country Club for good and he did not want to jeopardize his future. Guys like Barlew come and go. He was glad when Barlew did go, taking with him knowledge of the one-way mirror; Georgie felt a good deal more secure.

If he had had moral scruples about keeping tabs on the members in this way, they would have been driven away by reminding himself that employees were all but invisible to the members. Conversations that might stop or continue in a lowered voice at the approach of someone else went blithely on in the presence of Georgie and other employees. If he was invisible to them, there was no reason why they shouldn't be visible to him when he was absent. But Georgie had no scruples, at least of the ordinary kind. Listening to the members was not calculated to make him think he was wanting in a moral sensitivity prevalent in others. What crooks they all are, he would think, lolling in his chair and shaking his head. But it was envy and admiration rather than shock that he felt.

And there were sexual as well as financial shenanigans. Georgie was not as interested in these as Barlew had been but it would have been hard to be unaware of them. Mostly this information came indirectly. Some members talking about what some third member was up to. Georgie was no judge, but a lot of this sort of thing struck him as being imaginary. But then his attitude toward women was a mixture of the servile and the chivalrous. The truth was that Georgie had great difficulty imagining women doing what women are supposed to do with men. It was something outside his own experience. He had no curiosity about it. He really did not care to think about it. The usual masculine banter embarrassed him, giving him the sensation he was hearing a language he did not understand. His mother and Marion were not the kind of females on which he could have based a more romantic conception of the relation between the genders.

Georgie and Marion still lived with their mother. Marion, being retarded, had no choice. Maybe Georgie didn't either. When he had dreamed of moving into his hideaway at the clubhouse, sleeping there and everything, he had known it was an impossible dream. How could he leave Marion and his mother alone in the weather-beaten old house in Fox River that once, long ago, before Marion was born, had been a place of joy?

Marion was five years younger than Georgie, in years. Mentally, she was way down there, just a kid. A kid in a woman's body and that was one of the troubles. But long before that became a problem, Georgie's father disappeared, the year after Marion was born. Just went out of the house one morning and never came back. Both Georgie and his mother knew that Marion was the reason. His father could not accept that his daughter would never grow up mentally. Georgie remembered his father rocking Marion on the sun porch, tears just pouring from his eyes. Georgie's mother was ashamed of Marion too. When her husband took off, she seemed as angry that he had thought of the idea first as that he was gone.

Georgie had been happy to start working, part-time for years, a paper route first, then caddying. Almost from the start he had known that the Fox River Country Club was his destiny. The fact that he brought home money to his mother more than justified being away from the house. Georgie was ashamed of Marion too. And frightened by her. There was no telling when Marion was going to pull her dress over her head or do some awful thing that Georgie could not imagine any normal girl doing. Once he had waked up in the night to find that Marion had crawled in bed with him. He had let out a howl and his mother had come charging into the room. In that moment a celibate was born. And a romantic.

If his mother and sister provided no clue as to why men are attracted by women, the women at the club seemed desirable but inaccessible objects—perhaps desirable because inaccessible. No medieval monk had lived a life less carnal than Georgie's. But if Dante had his Beatrice and Petrarch his Laura, Georgie had Barbara Rooney. Once he had actually tried to write a poem about her, prompted by some fading memory of a high-school English class. He never finished it, it never got beyond four-and-a-half lines, but he didn't throw it away either. His idea had been to write seven lines, each of which would begin with the letters of her name.

> Because I always think of you
> Always think of me when you
> Remember how we fairways walked

> Beside each other, neither talked,
> And when we

It ended there. But he had written on the paper vertically the letters of her name, first and last, Barbara Rooney. If he ever finished the poem it would thus have thirteen lines which Georgie believed would make it a sonnet.

That he had even been able to make a start on a poem pleased and surprised him. He memorized these opening lines without realizing he was and, eyes closed, tipped back in his chair, he would repeat them to himself. The trouble with this was that he came to think of what he had already done as the complete poem, and this made it difficult to get back to work on it.

Why Barbara Rooney? She was an attractive, self-assured woman, but so were most of the women at the club. She played golf well, not a woman's game. She had a good swing and a good attitude. A bad shot, a bad hole, even a bad round did not destroy her. Next time. If she had a motto, that seemed to be it. Next time. Georgie had thought of this only in terms of her golf game but then he heard the locker room gossip. The talk was vague and full of snickers, with the emphasis more on what an ass her husband Frank was than on any misbehavior of hers. The idea seemed to be that, if she was doing something out of line, the real villain was Frank Rooney, not his wife Barbara. Georgie did not understand, he did not want to understand, the references to Mr. Rooney's competence as a husband. He was prepared to think Mr. Rooney was anything they wanted to call him. But he did not like dirty remarks being made about Barbara Rooney. Only Dr. Olson stood up for her and Georgie was so grateful to the dentist that he saw that his clubs were extra clean the next time he used them. It was the only way he could express his gratitude for what Olson had said. Not that the dentist's defense had been everything that Georgie might have desired.

"You guys are just jealous," Olson said. "Quit blaming Frank Rooney because Barbara won't look at you."

There was hooting and laughter and the painful snapping

of towels. Olson made a yipping retreat from the locker room. Georgie had noticed that the other men treated Dr. Olson as a comic character. He did look pretty funny trying to get out of the locker room while being pursued by half-a-dozen men snapping at his bare behind with wet towels. But for Georgie, Dr. Olson was the hero of that particular exchange, and the dentist had an extra clean set of golf clubs to prove it.

Needless to say, Barbara Rooney was completely unaware of the devotion she had inspired in Georgie. The possibility that she might find out and think him ridiculous or worse could make the sweat run down the sides of Georgie's body. Oh, sometimes he imagined being together with her, reciting to her his finished poem. The immediate sequel to this was unclear in his own mind, but his head felt dizzy at the thought and there was an odd constriction of his chest. But his poem remained unfinished and he contented himself with keeping a protective eye on her. He knew when she could be expected at the club. She golfed with both the eighteen-hole and nine-hole women's groups; perhaps once a week she golfed with her husband. And sometimes, on Thursdays, she golfed alone. On Thursdays Georgie made sweeping and unnecessary tours of the course, directing a golf cart through fairway and rough, keeping her in sight, but never getting close enough to be seen or to bother her game. It pleased him to think of himself as her protector. On these tours of the course his only concern was not to be noticed by Mrs. Rooney. It had never occurred to him that he might become a watched watcher.

"What are you?" Dr. Olson asked. "The pro-shop peeker?" The dentist was obviously angry but Georgie had no idea what he was talking about. Olson must have followed him to the hideaway, because Georgie had hardly shut the door when there was a knock on it. After his unintelligible question, Olson leaned into the room and whispered angrily. "Mrs. Rooney! Quit following her around, Georgie. I mean it."

Olson slammed the door shut and Georgie sat there, stunned, staring at his closed door. When his head cleared, he wanted to run after Olson and tell him they were on the same side, they felt the same way about Barbara Rooney. He didn't want Olson connecting him with those men who sat in the locker room and said bad things about her.

But he couldn't do that. He couldn't stop watching Barbara Rooney either, but from then on he was more careful, not wanting Olson to get the wrong idea about him. But the dentist seemed to know Georgie was still at it. From time to time Olson would look daggers at Georgie, as if to warn him. And then the worst possible thing happened.

Georgie came back to his hideaway to find Dr. Olson in his room. The dentist flourished the unfinished poem at Georgie, thus depriving him of the chance of being the wronged party here.

"What the hell is this, Georgie?"

"Give me that."

Olson pulled back the paper and put it behind him. "I told you to cut it out, Georgie. I meant it."

"Don't show that to anyone. Give it to me. I'll do whatever you say."

"You're damned right you will, Georgie." Olson brought the poem from behind his back and began to read it, a disgusted look on his face. Then he marched out of the room, taking the poem with him. Georgie had never felt so awful in his life.

5

ANGELA had switched from Manhattans to sweet rob roys because Manhattans reminded her too forcibly of Barbara. She had thought of stopping drinking entirely but that was at least as depressing a prospect as quitting smoking. Endless time seemed to stretch before her, an arid desert, herself crawling from mirage to mirage. She and Barbara had consoled each other because of their inability to stop smoking. It was so dumb to go on smoking. It was crazy to think, each time she lit one, that soon she would give them up. Now with Barbara dead, it seemed foolish to speak of the rest of her life as if that were an endless time. Barbara had thought she had all the time in the world too, and look at what happened to her.

Angela stubbed out her cigarette and sipped her drink. Josephine the bartender was at the far end doing her nails. Somewhere in the darkness behind, a couple whispered at their table. It was two-thirty in the afternoon. Soon the bunch would begin to arrive and the place would liven up. This was Angela's place, the Gutter Ball, named thus because of its proximity to a bowling alley. For Barbara it had been slumming to come here but Angela was only comfortable in this kind of place. Once she had favored the bar at the country club, but after the divorce, she just did not want to risk running into Jerry.

He had taken the divorce badly. He still thought she would come back to him. He couldn't talk about it without tearing, and if he had a drink, he became absolutely maudlin. Maybe she had been divorcing the club as much as Jerry. For him, being a member represented something truly special. Not many Jews were members of the Fox River Country Club. How could he stand the hypocrisy? But Jerry was so nice a man he probably did not think there was much difference between the public and private lives of the other members. But basically Angela had just grown tired of cheating on Jerry. The divorce was her blow against hypocrisy. She just dropped the pretense of being a faithful wife, admitted to herself and others that she liked hanging around places like the Gutter Ball half the day and half the night as well. The word she preferred to describe her conduct was "promiscuous." It had a nice whistling sound to it and besides, it suggested that she was the way she was because of her genes rather than choice.

"Want me to freshen that up, Angie?" Josephine came from the other end of the bar holding her hands out before her as if she were going to bring them down on a keyboard. The smell of nail polish was pungent in the air.

"In a minute."

"You two all right back there?" Josephine called into the gloom. There was a negative grumble. Josephine leaned over the bar and whispered out of the side of her mouth. "What they need is more ice. You know where. I'd like to have a switch here so that I could throw on the lights from time to time. God only knows what goes on back there in the dark."

"Oh, come on, Jo. You know what happens in the dark."

"Yeah. But we don't have that kind of license." Jo stepped back, waving her hands, drying the polish.

"Has it really been a week?" Angela nodded. A week since Barbara was murdered in her bath. They all agreed that it had to be murder. The day Barbara Rooney killed herself was the day water ran up hill. Maybe the others in the Gutter Ball didn't know Barb well enough to say that, but Angela did; they had been close for years, veterans of the country club bar. There were some people you know right away are on the same frequency and Barb and Angie had hit it off from the start. Angie found the answer to that.

"We're both Libra. That's why we're so much alike."

"If you believe in signs, we're very different. That's all superstitious."

Angela only smiled. She had heard that one before. Maybe all Barb knew was the kind of column carried in the *Fox River Messenger*. But if she needed proof that signs influence our lives, Angela was sure she could provide it. But Barbara was stubbornly resistant. No wonder. She had been raised a Catholic.

"Speaking of superstition," Angela said carefully, and was relieved when Barb laughed.

"I said that was the way I was raised. I'm a big girl now." A flicker of sadness passed across her face. "Big enough to see the crutch astrology is."

Angela let it go. Barb would see the light. She had to. It was in the stars.

A week since she was killed. The fact that she had been killed in midmorning made the thing scarier. Angela wanted to think that she was safe when the sun shone and people were busy everywhere. But someone had walked into Barb's house, come upstairs, and killed her. Angela shivered, causing the ice to tinkle in her glass, and Josephine came and took it.

"More of the same?"

Angela nodded. Thank God the Gutter Ball was dark. Tears leaked from her eyes at the vivid reminder of how often she and Barbara Rooney had sat drinking away the afternoon like this. It wasn't fair that a person who had been so much fun should be dead. At the time it must have happened, Angela was still asleep. It was a wonder Barbara hadn't been killed in bed, asleep, considering the night the two of them had had.

That Tuesday afternoon they had been sitting right here at the bar of the Gutter Ball. At five Barb would begin to make the first moves toward leaving; that was the way it usually was. She had to get home. But that night five o'clock came and Barb stayed comfortable on her stool. Finally Angela said something. She loved to talk with Barb but as a friend she could not ignore Barb's need to get home.

"Not tonight. Francis X. is out of town. Gone to a reunion at a school he claims to hate. I can sit right here as long as I want."

Angela called for another round and they drank to Barb's freedom.

"Queen for a night," Barbara said, lifting her glass.

"Who, Frank?"

"I've told you, Angie, that isn't true. He has lots of faults, like the rest of us, but that is not among them. So what shall we do tonight?"

The key to a good time is to keep planning to a minimum. This was a truth Angela had learned the hard way. The more you planned, the greater your expectations and the greater the possibility of disappointment. Far better to play it loose, move with the flow, see what happened. If nothing did, okay, there is always tomorrow.

Barbara agreed, as she had on previous such occasions. She got more comfortable at the bar of the Gutter Ball.

Nothing happened until they went on for dinner at Tim's. They were bound to meet people they knew there, of course, but they went anyway. That they might be open to whatever turned up remained unspoken between them and Angie hadn't wanted to veto Tim's just because some friends of theirs might be among the diners there. And so there were. If Martin Olson can be called a friend. He was no friend of Angie's, not after all the work he had done in her mouth.

"Well, if it isn't my favorite oral surgeon," Angie said when Martin crossed the room to their table. He didn't seem to hear her. No doubt this was because of the acoustics in Tim's. Martin hovered over their table, the intrepid foe of decay and gum disorders. There was such a pitiable look on his face as he asked to join them that Angie was all for it and said so. He pulled out a chair swiftly, as if he were performing a magic trick, and sat down.

"The headwaiter says I'd have to wait over an hour to get a single."

"You're eating alone?" Angie said. What a sad thought, Martin Olson alone with his dinner while all around him festive diners added to his despair with their laughter and banter.

"Bachelors often do," Martin said. He smiled brightly but it seemed clearly a brave front.

"You might ask someone to join you," Barbara said. "Of course it would cost you money. This is Dutch treat, by the way. It won't cost you a cent."

"Just ask someone out. You make it sound easy."

"It is. Ask Angie out."

Red shone on Martin's cheeks when he turned to Angie.

"Don't you dare," Angie said. "Tonight can be our date." So Martin Olson ate with them. It wasn't any fun at all, it was difficult to say why, it just wasn't.

After dinner, in the rest room, Angie realized that she had accepted Martin Olson at the table on the assumption that he was a friend of Barbara's and vice versa.

"My friend?" Barbara laughed. "He's my dentist, not my friend. I thought that you..."

"You're kidding. Martin Olson? Me?" Angie hoped her dismissive laughter sounded convincing. The guilty truth was that she had gone out with Martin.

It had been a dance at the country club and Angie had accepted because Jerry was out of town and there was no danger she would suddenly find herself confronting his sad, accusing eyes from behind some potted palm. Why had she accepted? The answer to that was: Why not? Martin Olson wasn't her idea of a barrel of laughs, but he was a man and the dance could turn out to be fun. It turned out like a high-school prom, with Martin never quite sure what he was supposed to do. This was annoying at first but then it took on its own kind of charm. It was incredible that a man Martin's age, and a very successful man, to the degree that success is a matter of money, knew so little about what to do at a dance, what to do with a woman. Martin was such an earnest, unhumorous man that it took a while for his ineptitude to bring out the mother in Angie. The thought of being an earth mother and presiding over Martin's initiation appealed to her. Incredible as it seemed, Angie was willing to bet that Martin was a virgin. To be the seducer rather than the seduced had its somewhat perverse appeal. But the evening gave Angie some insight into a man's plight in such matters. The thought that she could be willing and Martin unwilling had not occurred to her. Perhaps "uncomprehending" was a better word for him.

One of the curiosities of their date had been the fact that Angie had driven her own car to the club. Martin's appointments were running late and she told him, no problem, we can meet there. Afterward, she did not want to leave her car in the parking lot of the club, so she told Martin to meet her at her place. It was possible that he did not understand the invitation. Or that he did and got cold feet and decided not to come. Angie never found out. He never asked her out again. They never talked about the dance. All in all, it had been a deflating experience. Angie was not prepared for the thought that she could be turned down by Martin Olson. She had never told anyone about it until the night Martin asked if he could join her and Barbara. When things became clear in the Ladies Room, they decided to free themselves of the company of Martin Olson.

They returned to the Gutter Ball and it was there, sitting in the dimly lit but now crowded bar, that Angie told Barbara of her odd date with Martin Olson. Barbara didn't laugh, thank God.

"He doesn't understand discouragement either, Angela."

"Oh?"

"It's a long story."

"So. We're in no rush."

Angela felt that Barbara had been leading Martin on, maybe without realizing it. She should have seen that something was afoot when Olson himself did the series of checkups after her oral surgery. And monthly checkups for a year? She had to be kidding. No wonder Martin tried to make a move. And what a move.

"He asked me to marry him. Just like that. Leave Frank and the kids and run away with him. He proposed this while he was flossing my teeth."

"You were in a dental chair at the time!"

"Where else would he be flossing my teeth? Let me tell you, it puts you at a disadvantage to be asked something like that when you're tipped back arse over teakettle and the man has his hands in your mouth."

"What did you do?"

"Closed my eyes, shook my head, and listened to my saliva burble through the tube."

"Did he try anything?"

Barbara laughed for an answer to that and, given her own experience, Angie believed her. What a jerk Martin Olson was. But he served his purpose, talk of him leading on to other things. Angie was frank if a little oblique about her life-style and Barbara did not pretend to be shocked. They hit it off. As they had before, Angie knew that she and Barbara would have a good time with Frank Rooney out of town.

Last Tuesday night, Barbara Rooney's last night on earth, they had had quite a time. They met two guys at the Gutter Ball and went on eventually to Angie's. There had been a lot of drinking, before, during, and after. Until the awful news of Barbara's murder came, Angie's memories of that night were vague and warm and satisfied. After she learned of Barbara's death, after the initial shock, she had lived in dread that someone was going to mention having seen Barbara out on the town with Angela Sykes and she would be all over the newspapers. Suddenly she knew that, however much of a free spirit she chose to be, she did not want to flaunt the way she lived. Besides, she was bound to be asked about the men she and Barbara were with, and the fact was that Angie did not know who they were. She didn't even know the name of the man she had been with.

Early in the evening she had started to call him Woodie, for Woodie Woodpecker, because of his pointed nose. The man Barbara had been with was called Ollie. He was tall and broad and in very fine physical shape. Maybe that is what appealed to Barbara Rooney, she was such a sportswoman herself.

The whole story was ludicrous and cast no light on Barbara's death. Ollie had been gentle, no matter his size, and he had been a perfect gentleman. Besides, he and Woodie were gone by four and Barbara left after that. Angela assured herself that, if telling of that night could help find Barbara's murderer, she would go to the police immediately. She wouldn't care if it was embarrassing to her. But she was positive there was no connection between Ollie and Woodie and Barbara's horrible death. Angie wondered if either of the two men had read of her death and made a connection between their night of dalliance and the murdered woman.

"I couldn't attend the funeral," Josephine said.

"You didn't miss anything."

"I can't stand them," Josephine said, her voice almost a whine. "Not since my mother's. Did I ever tell you of my mother's funeral?"

She did then and Angie more or less tuned her out. It didn't seem right, using Barbara's funeral as an excuse to talk of another. Barbara's had been a very bleak, sad affair.

Angela had expected a Catholic thing, Mass, procession to the cemetery, priest blessing the grave. But there was only Hawks from the funeral home and he read a poem Angie didn't recognize as if he expected to be arrested at any moment for impersonating a clergyman. Other people there seemed as surprised as Angie. She wished someone would ask Frank Rooney why, but no one did. Angie didn't either. She was a fine one to seemingly criticize him for not giving a church funeral. Besides, Frank seemed so different. And not just the difference due to what he had been through. Martin Olson did not get out of his car and come to the grave. When she went back to her car, Angela noticed him sitting behind the wheel of his. He looked up at her, startled when she went by. His eyes were full of tears.

6

PHIL KEEGAN nodded and held out his cup for a refill. Cy Horvath
poured coffee with the same singleness of purpose with which he performed any task. After replacing the Mr. Coffee pot, Cy resumed
his seat across from Captain Keegan's desk. They were in the process
of reviewing the Barbara Rooney death, in search of something solid
with which to stop Robertson from asking Phelps to bring in a verdict of suicide. The chief had suddenly decided that Frank Rooney's
feelings were not as important as getting an unexplained death off
the record. Keegan had spent the morning with Robertson and felt
that he had been trying to communicate with a native of another,
and lesser, planet.

"How did she cut her wrists?" he had asked Robertson.

"Did you have the drain of the tub checked?" the chief
asked, looking shrewd. Phil Keegan had long since ceased thinking
of himself as an objective observer of Robertson, so the fact that he

thought the chief acquired a simian look whenever he attempted to convey the thought that he knew something about police work had to be discounted somewhat. Robertson seemed to think the razor had gone down the drain. The drain that had been plugged. It gave Keegan no satisfaction to tell Robertson that, yes, they had checked the drain.

"As a routine matter. We didn't expect to find anything, and we didn't."

"It doesn't matter."

"It does if you want a rational explanation of the woman's death." One of the annoying aspects of Robertson's stupidity was the fact that the man could not be insulted.

"We can't be wasting time and men and resources on it. I am going to speak to Phelps."

"What's the rush? Give me a week."

"You buy Rooney's story about the aluminum-siding salesman?"

Rooney had suddenly remembered that his wife had been frightened by a pushy salesman in a truck who had tried to talk her into new aluminum doors for the house. Keegan was not impressed by that possibility, but apparently it worried Robertson.

"We should follow up on it," Keegan said.

Robertson had given him five days, which was as good as a week. Now the question was how best to use the time they had gained. Keegan looked at Cy Horvath. "You're sure you don't want to throw in the towel, Cy?"

Keegan had worked closely with Cy for years and he still could not discern any change of expression on the Lieutenant's broad Slavic face. Nonetheless, he knew that Cy did not like to be asked pointless questions. They both knew that the death of Barbara Rooney involved a crime and neither of them could rest content while crimes committed in Fox River, Illinois, went undetected and unprosecuted. Robertson was a politician; the people in the district attorney's office were politicians. They might have to respond to outside pressures. But for Keegan and Horvath life was simpler. They were in the business of investigating crimes and apprehending criminals. Simpler. Not easier.

"You think he did it?"

"He was out of town when it happened." He looked at Keegan, the remark as much a question as a statement. Cy wanted to know if they had any reason to doubt Rooney's claim to have been at an alumni reunion in Wisconsin.

"We'll assume he's accounted for, Cy. You still want to question him some more?"

Cy nodded. "I don't understand him. Did he hate his wife or what? He wants to protect her good name, it seems. No suicide. Okay. The devoted husband. Does he seem really grieved to you?"

Keegan shrugged. He had lost his own wife, to cancer, not to violence. How had he acted at the time? He recalled a period of numbness and disbelief. That might have struck others as callous. Grief is not a single thing.

"If it's murder and the husband is out, what do we have? The bushy-haired stranger?"

"All we've got is Barbara Rooney. What was she really like?"

"Go find out."

Cy got up immediately. His motion if not his expression indicated he was relieved to be given a go-ahead. When the door closed behind Horvath, Keegan stood and picked up his phone and dialed the number of St. Hilary's rectory.

"You said you know someone at the school Rooney attended in Wisconsin?"

"You must know him too. Chrysostom Pine. He was a member of my class." Keegan didn't remember him.

"If I took a run up there, could you come along? I figure that with luck the round-trip drive will take three-and-a-half, four hours. Say an hour or so there, we could be back in time for dinner."

"You're talking about today?"

"I'd rather not put it off, but it could hold until tomorrow."

"Today is as good as tomorrow for me, Phil. But wouldn't it be easier to make a few phone calls? I could phone Chris and you can get in touch with the local police there."

"I'd feel better if I saw the place."

"Has something come up?"

"No, it's just routine. I mean it. Maybe it's not a necessary trip. The only way I can be sure of that is by going up there."

There was a pause on the other end of the line. Finally Roger Dowling said, "What time were you thinking of leaving?"

It was going on eleven when they left Fox River, heading east on I-94 to the junction where they could turn north. The interstate is largely a seasonless road; their prospect was one of concrete and steel to the degree they had a prospect. The traffic was heavy and they were soon hemmed in by semis. Even with the windows of the car closed, the noise was horrendous. Near O'Hare, a steady stream of landing planes added to the busyness of the day. Roger sat silently in the passenger seat, puffing on his pipe, seemingly content to have a break from routine. There was no point trying to carry on a conversation until they cleared this congestion, and they were good enough friends to be comfortable with silence.

Keegan now had opportunity to wonder if it had been wise to enlist Roger's help on this errand. It might be significant that the only one he would have told of it was Cy Horvath. Imagine Robertson's reaction if he knew his chief of detectives was conducting inquiries in the company of the pastor of St. Hilary's. But Keegan had learned from experience that Roger Dowling could be a good person to have along on such occasions.

Last night they had talked in Roger's study. Keegan was looking for a culprit, but Roger Dowling was looking for someone in flight from God, someone in need of mercy. It was confusing that they were after the same person on such occasions. Keegan was not sure how punishment and forgiveness could go to the same person for the same reason. Well, he would leave such complicated thinking to people like Dowling. The priest could afford the luxury of regarding criminals as lost sheep in need only of the Good Shepherd to straighten out their lives. Keegan knew better. Killers were likely to kill again. Criminals became adept at manipulating those impulses to forgive that most people have — above all: parole boards, sitting judges, and some juries. As far as Keegan was concerned, forgiveness could wait for the next life. He told Dowling as much.

"And reward too?"

Keegan had gone into the kitchen of the rectory for another bottle of beer. He did not want to argue the matter with the priest. In fact, he was glad there were people like Roger around. All he knew was that he could not adopt the priest's attitude and be much of a cop. Nor did he think that meant he wasn't a Christian.

"I would never say that about you, Phil."

Maybe that was why his studies for the priesthood had been aborted. Maybe the trouble he had with Latin was not the full story. Keegan had remained devout; his devotion had even increased since the death of his wife and his renewed friendship with Roger Dowling. Often he attended the Mass Roger Dowling said each weekday at noon.

"Who will say the noon Mass?" he asked when they had turned north and were headed away from Chicago and intense traffic. On either side of the highway, posh suburbs sat among clouds of trees splendid with autumnal colors.

"Father Placidus. From the retreat house."

A Franciscan! Keegan did not like Franciscans, he was not quite sure why. Roger was asking where the investigation into Barbara Rooney's death was.

"Nowhere. Robertson wants to wrap it up, call it a suicide, forget it. We have five days to come up with good reasons to stop that."

"This trip suggests you think Francis Rooney might be responsible."

"Well, I want to make sure he couldn't have been. If he was in Wisconsin, okay. He couldn't have done it. Not unless he could..." Keegan paused. "What's that word?"

"Bilocate?"

"Yeah. Maybe saints can do that but murderers are in one place at a time."

"He is a very odd man, Frank Rooney. He asked me to bless his wife's grave."

Keegan snorted. "Why didn't he have a regular funeral?" Dowling didn't answer, but Keegan knew the answer to that one. Neither Rooney nor his wife had seen the inside of a church for years.

Dowling said, "Did you have a man at the burial?"

"Cy Horvath was there."

"What was it like?"

"Someone read a poem. Then they took the body to the cemetery and that was that. And then he thinks to have her grave blessed?"

"I wonder who the mourners were?"

Keegan shrugged.

"Lieutenant Horvath would remember, wouldn't he?" Roger already knew the answer to that. "How did she live, Phil? What were her days like?"

As far as Phil knew, the life Barbara Rooney had led would suggest to most people, himself included, a perpetual vacation. She played games and ate and went to parties. When this rigorous life grew wearisome, she renewed herself with travel, to Florida, Hawaii, Europe.

"She must have been bored to death, Phil."

"I don't know. I've never lived that way."

"You should thank God for that. In the *Summa Theologiae*, Saint Thomas says that the best proof that such a life cannot satisfy us is had when we try to lead it. Can you imagine trying to live for the sake of fun?"

Keegan kept his eyes on the road and did not smile. Roger Dowling was always assuming he knew things he didn't. St. Thomas and the *Summa*? Robertson should overhear such a conversation.

7

THERE were several reasons why Roger Dowling accepted Phil Keegan's invitation to come with him to Wisconsin. He had told Mrs. Murkin it was a chance to see his old classmate Chrysostom Pine.

"I've never heard you mention him."

"I haven't seen him for years. That's the point." He realized that he seemed to be apologizing to Marie. She certainly had not responded kindly to the news that Father Placidus would say the noon Mass and have lunch in the rectory.

"Father Placidus! Didn't they have anyone else free?"

Marie complained that Placidus treated her as if she were a waitress on the few occasions when he came to fill in for the pastor of St. Hilary's. A Mass and a lunch were bad enough, but last summer Placidus had taken over for two weeks while Roger Dowling was on vacation. He had returned to find a silent and resentful housekeeper. The sad tale had come out over the course of several weeks.

Placidus had given Marie Murkin unsolicited spiritual advice. He had particularly admonished her for the curiosity she showed in visitors to the rectory. And he claimed that he could hear her television and it bothered him. Nor could she satisfy him at table. Not that she tried very hard after the first few days. Placidus had been fed what in Marie Murkin's mind was close to prison fare before the two weeks were up. The surprising thing was that Father Placidus had only good things to say of Marie Murkin. Father Dowling reminded her of that before Phil Keegan came to call for him.

"Words are cheap," the housekeeper humphed.

Another reason to go with Phil was simply to take a break.

Roger Dowling loved his life at St. Hilary's. His daily routine was a source of contentment and joy. Sometimes he felt guilty at the thought that his life was so much more fulfilling and pleasant than it had been before his assignment to St. Hilary's. But happy as he was, he did not want to get into a rut, and a day away from the rectory could be a way of insuring that he would do his work there better.

A third reason was the real reason he was riding northward to Wisconsin with Phil Keegan.

Francis X. Rooney was indeed a strange fellow. He had come for Roger Dowling on the day the priest had blessed Barbara Rooney's grave.

The cemetery was glorious with color and the fallen leaves scattered on the lawn and adorning the monuments made it difficult to think of it as a sad place. Nor did Rooney induce somber thoughts. He whistled a little tuneless whistle as he drove, interrupting himself only to make a vacuous remark about the weather. They parked on a narrow road in the cemetery and Rooney led the way across the lawn.

He could not find his wife's grave. The spot to which he had walked was not her grave; he looked back toward his car, a puzzled expression on his face, trying to get his bearings. He began to wander around, looking for fresh graves, but none was Barbara Rooney's.

"I know it's around here someplace."

"Does it have a marker?"

"I ordered one."

"I don't suppose it's been made yet. Maybe you should go to the office and get directions."

Rooney had not liked the suggestion that he did not know where his wife was buried. In the end he did drive to the cemetery office to discover the location of the grave. Roger Dowling waited for him, enjoying the rustling serenity of the place. How final was this final resting place? Burial grounds of past civilizations were treasure troves to archeologists. Was it fanciful to imagine that in some unimaginable future this place would be an object of scholarly attention, searched for clues as to what it had been like in the twentieth century? What would these steel boxes with their inner-spring mattresses and waterproof vaults tell those future men of the present? Would the care with which we bury our dead suggest a belief in resurrection or a repudiation of it? Brittle leaves spun down from brittle branches as commentary on these pleasantly somber thoughts. When Rooney returned, it emerged that they had come to the wrong section of the grounds.

Eventually the two men stood at Barbara Rooney's grave, the widower and the priest. Roger Dowling read the service and sprinkled holy water on the grave. Frank Rooney did not seem to know what to do when Father Dowling handed him the silver phial.

"Just shake some water on the grave."

"Father, don't misunderstand. I'm doing this for Barbara. You mustn't think I still believe..." Rooney stopped, as if his disbelief were a discourtesy rather than a tragedy. On the ride back to St. Hilary's, he went on about it.

"I don't even remember what it was like to believe, Father. Maybe I never did. It was just routine. You know."

"I know. Like having your wife's grave blessed."

"That's different. That's for her." Rooney shrugged. "It seemed the right thing to do. Who knows? Maybe she still believed some of it. It can't hurt anything, can it?"

"What was your wife like?"

"She was an excellent wife and mother." Rooney spoke quickly and with no apparent doubt.

"What will happen to the children?"

"What do you mean?" Rooney looked sharply at Roger Dowling.

"Can you raise them yourself?"

"If necessary I shall hire whatever help I need."

"Maybe you will remarry someday."

Rooney thought about that. Apparently he did not find the suggestion offensive or inappropriate.

"That's true."

Frank Rooney was an enigma. Father Dowling did not understand him. Was he shallow or deep? Maybe a look at his old school would give some clue to the man.

The school was located on wooded grounds and was reached by a long road winding among the trees. The main building was of brick with a Spanish tile roof. The road described a circle in front of the entrance and Phil Keegan parked. Almost immediately an officious youth appeared beside the car. He tapped on the window and Phil Keegan rolled it down.

"You can't park here, sir. Visitors' parking is over there." He pointed without turning his pimply face from Phil Keegan.

"Are you a student here?" Phil asked.

The boy reddened. "I am the school prefect."

"Do you have some identification?"

"My name is Hanke. Jerome Hanke."

"What if I told you that I'm Senator Proxmire and this is Cardinal Dowling?"

The boy stepped back. "I'm sorry, Senator. I didn't recognize you."

"I'm lying, Jerome. How do I get to visitors' parking?"

A confused school prefect led the way for him. Roger Dowling said nothing. He did not approve of Phil's teasing the boy like that. When he got out of the car, he asked Jerome where he could find Father Pine.

Chris had rooms in Pitner Residence. Jerome would be glad to show him where. Phil went off to the main building to interview the headmaster.

"You're not a cardinal, are you?" Jerome asked when they were alone.

"Good heavens, no." And he did feel relieved at having only the humblest clerical status.

Chris was surprisingly unchanged from decades before. His blond hair seemed untouched with gray, his blue eyes twinkled, and his face was unlined save for the smile with which he greeted Roger Dowling.

"Roger, how's the marriage court?" Chris asked when Dowling had thanked Jerome for his help and taken the comfortable chair to which Chris waved him.

"I'm no longer on it, Chris. I have a little parish west of Chicago."

"I hadn't heard. What will you have to drink?"

"Nothing. Thank you. But go ahead, Chris."

Some memory seemed to stir in Chris's eyes. Perhaps he had heard of the fall of Roger Dowling after all.

"You had a reunion here recently, didn't you, Chris? I wonder if you know a man named Frank Rooney. He came up for the occasion."

Chris had lighted a cigarette. He tipped back his head and directed a thin stream of smoke at the ceiling. "Rooney? I don't remember. There are hundreds who came back, Roger. I know quite a few of them, of course, particularly those who come back often. Many of them I knew as students here. What class was Rooney in?"

"I think he said it was his thirtieth anniversary."

"Before my time then. What do you want to know about him?"

"If he was here for the reunion."

"Ah. I can check with the alumni office. Should I?"

Roger Dowling said yes and Chris picked up his phone and dialed. Francis X. Rooney had registered for the reunion. Since he had decided to come at the last moment he had not been assigned a room on campus. With several dozen others he had been put up in a motel in the town.

"Is there some doubt he came, Roger?"

"His wife died while he was here. It appears that she was murdered. You don't remember a Phil Keegan, do you? No, you wouldn't have known him. He was a class behind us at Quigley, but you didn't attend Quigley, did you?"

"Just Mundelein."

"Keegan is chief of detectives in Fox River. He is investigating the death of Rooney's wife. I mentioned I had a classmate here and he asked me to come along. I hoped you knew Frank Rooney."

"If anyone would, I would. Do you know I am the senior person on the staff? There is always quite a turnover at a place like this. That and retirements have left me like the servant in Job. The only survivor. If I don't know Rooney, no one does. But what a horrible thing about his wife."

The conversation turned quickly to clerical gossip, to talk of other classmates, to memories of their shared youth. How long had it been since they had seen each other? At least a quarter of a century. It didn't seem to matter. It helped that Chris was so unchanged in appearance, but basically it was clerical camaraderie.

Reinforced by the fact that they had been classmates. And Chris was genuinely interested in St. Hilary's. "It doesn't sound too demanding, Roger."

"It keeps me busy."

"I've been kidded a lot about this job. Chaplain to spoiled rich kids. Not exactly the life one looked forward to in the seminary. But this is where my bishop sent me and I do what I can. These are important years in a boy's life, Roger. Remember your early teens?"

"I do indeed. Painfully."

"Exactly. Kids that age go through agonies. It is easy for adults to dismiss their problems as silly. But those are the problems they have."

Roger Dowling wondered what life had been like here for Francis Rooney. As he talked with Chris, sounds of drilling cadets drifted to them from the parade grounds behind the field. It seemed a regimented life for boys. How sad to be separated from parents and family. Well, Rooney had said he hated it.

"He was here, all right," Phil said later.

Chris had taken Roger Dowling to the administration building where the alumni office was located. Keegan seemed to be sizing Chris up after Roger Dowling introduced him to his classmate.

"Playing soldier," was his general comment on the school. He shook his head. "It seems a waste of a priest to stick him away in a place like this." They were headed down the road that had brought them to the administration building an hour-and-a-half earlier.

"There is always work for a priest to do."

"And a cop."

"They remember Rooney at the reunion?"

"He had registered. He signed up for several workshops on Tuesday afternoon and for another early Wednesday morning."

"How early?"

"Eight. Do you know they have reveille at quarter of six? Around here, eight is like noon."

"Didn't Rooney discover his wife's body at eleven?"

"If he left here at nine, he could have been home by then. I want to find out when he checked out of his motel."

Rooney had stayed in the Holiday Inn at the southern edge of town. The manager considered Phil Keegan's badge and I.D., he glanced with a frown at Roger Dowling's Roman collar. He seemed at a loss. How should he react to the appearance of an out-of-town policeman and a thin, pipe-smoking priest at his counter? He seemed to decide that cooperation committed him to nothing.

"What were the dates again?"

Phil repeated the days earlier in the month when Frank Rooney had stayed in the motel. The manager found his registration card.

"Do you have a photocopier here?"

"You want a copy of this?"

"I'll pay for it."

"Oh, it isn't that." The manager sought to negate his baldness by sweeping hair from the side of his head over the top and spraying it into submission. Beneath his thin nose an enormous mustache flourished. It twitched as index to his indecision.

"The Academy gave me copies of Rooney's registration for the reunion. Would you like to see them? This is an official investigation, Mr. Crock."

"Krich. *K-R-I-C-H.*" He indicated the name plate on the counter which bore these letters. "Very well, if the Academy allowed you to make copies I suppose I can do the same."

He took his time about it. Phil grumbled at the desk. He hoped to beat the worst of the traffic on the drive home and Krich's dallying didn't help. Roger Dowling looked around the lobby, low-ceilinged, comfortable if fragile-looking furniture, lamps hanging from looped chains over chairs and couches. The note of transiency was eased by the fact that exact duplicates of the motel could be found throughout the country.

When Krich returned with a photocopy of Rooney's registration, Phil said, "He checked out on the Wednesday morning."

"As you can see, he paid in advance. There was no need for him to check out."

"So you couldn't vouch for the fact that he spent that night here."

"I can vouch for the fact that he registered and paid for a room." Krich's face suddenly assumed a look of panic. "I'm not going to be called to testify, am I?"

"To what?"

"You said this was an official investigation."

"It's up to the prosecutor to issue subpoenas."

They left Krich wringing his hands at the thought that he might have to journey to Illinois to verify the record he had provided Phil Keegan.

"Do you doubt that Rooney spent the night here, Phil?"

"He was there bright and early for an eight-o'clock meeting. And he had breakfast in the school refectory. That began at six-thirty. No, Rooney was here. There's no doubt about that. Look at this damned traffic."

And thus in silence they were enveloped by the hurtling traffic that bore them southward and eventually home. Frank Rooney had returned to Fox River on this road, not suspecting he was returning as a widower to a murdered wife.

8

CY HORVATH did not smolder with proletarian resentment when he drove through the entrance of the Fox River Country Club and wound beneath trees toward the white buildings visible ahead. Fallen leaves drifted across the road like golden snow and there was the scent of smoke in the air. Neither was he overwhelmed by nostalgia at this familiar scene rendered unfamiliar by the season and the passage of years. Cy had caddied here as a boy. It was an occupation he remembered as indolent and leisurely rather than demeaning. Long lazy hours spent in the shade of the caddy shack, early Monday mornings when the course had been open to the caddies, the welcome income from a healthy outdoor job.

He followed the road around the tennis courts and swimming pool. To the left, in a hollow, was the building that once had been the caddy shack but was now used to house some of the golf carts that had replaced the boys. Fairways, still green, stretched away into the distance, inviting escape. This had been the almost daily setting of Barbara Rooney's life and Cy Horvath meant to find out as much about the woman as he could.

He had trusted Captain Keegan to resist the course Robertson was urging. Now that they had been given at least a week to do it, he meant to do his part to make a monkey out of the police chief. If Barbara Rooney's death was not a murder, Cy Horvath was ready to, well, go back to caddying. They had very little on the woman so far. Her husband was a worthless source and, going by the funeral, she had few close friends. Cy had noticed Angela Sykes there. That was a small surprise, given Angela's reputation, when she went on to the cemetery.

One thing about being a cop, you found out which of the most respectable citizens led a secret life, catting around town. Angie stayed out of trouble, there had never been an arrest, though there could have been many. She insisted on driving herself and that meant she was on the streets, drunk, when she headed home in the early hours of the morning. The night patrols became solicitous of people like Angela Sykes, convoying them through the early-morning streets, hoping they didn't sideswipe a parked car. The fact that Angie hung around the Gutter Ball said it all, at least if you were a cop. The place was notorious as a hangout for the divorced or straying. Cabbies put passing salesmen onto the place as a bar where contacts could be made. And Angela made her contacts. What had Angela to do with Barbara Rooney? The question remained even after Cy found out that both women had belonged to the country club. It was the country club Cy was counting on to give him the beginnings of a picture of the life Barbara Rooney had led.

He parked at an angle in front of the entrance. It was midmorning, too early for the arrival of those who would have lunch at the club. When he got out and slammed the door of the car, the sound seemed to go over the pool and tennis courts and move out the fairway, lost in the vastness. The steps leading up to the entrance were covered with artificial turf which looked unnaturally green in the morning light. Inside, Cy found empty rooms. He walked across the polished wooden floors in the direction of a muffled noise. On an enclosed veranda, a black of medium height was using a floor polisher. His eyes were closed and he moved with his machine as if it were his dancing partner. Horvath stopped and waited for the man to open his eyes. A minute passed and the strange minuet continued. Horvath went to the wall and unplugged the machine. The man's eyes opened and Cy showed him his shield.

"Who's in charge here?"

"In charge of what? I'm the only one working. Unless you mean the manager. He's on through there, off the bar."

"Thanks."

"Ain't you going to plug me in again?"

Horvath smiled. "Sure. Sorry to interrupt."

Plugged in, the polisher began again to wail and the man once more closed his eyes and directed the machine rhythmically over the floor.

The manager's office was at right angles to the bar. The brass plate screwed onto the door read: Randolph G. Anvers, Mgr. Cy knocked and then looked around the bar. The room was a semi-circular one and the bar bellied into the room, its arc matching that of the room's outer wall. The furniture in the room was maple and the curtains at the window suggested a kitchen rather than a bar to Horvath. A sort of canopy covered the bar. The maple stools had red checkered cushions. Horvath could not imagine enjoying a drink there. The door behind him opened and he turned to face a very fat man of middle height whose glasses had been pushed back to rest on his head. The lenses of the glasses were as expressive as his eyes. Cy showed his shield.

"I'd like to talk with you about Barbara Rooney, Mr. Anvers."

"No. I never talk about members or their wives. I suggest

you speak with the club president or members of the governing board. I simply work here."

"We can sit here," Cy suggested, drawing a chair out from one of the tables and sitting down. Anvers, who had come out of his office, shutting the door behind him, stared at Horvath.

"I have nothing to say, Lieutenant."

"That's pretty good."

"What do you mean?"

"Guessing my rank. You had maybe five seconds glance and you saw that I was a lieutenant. You are a very observant person, Mr. Anvers."

It is the rare person who is unmoved by praise. Anvers was not among them. But he tried to be. "Now, don't you start flattering me, Lieutenant."

"I won't. Flattery is either false or an exaggeration. I merely state a fact. Sit down. This won't take long."

Anvers pulled out a chair and lowered a fraction of his behind onto it. His sigh was either one of resignation or an effect of the physical effort.

"I warn you, I have nothing to say that will be of the least help to you."

"You think the murder of Barbara Rooney is insoluble? You may be right."

"Murder!" Anvers seemed genuinely surprised. "I thought it was suicide."

"What made you think that?"

Anvers brought a package of cigarettes from the inside pocket of his suit jacket which he had unbuttoned before sitting down. He shook a cigarette free and put it in a corner of his mouth. Horvath waited while he lit it. Anvers said through a cloud of smoke, "I didn't *think* it was suicide. That was the story around here."

"Does that sound plausible to you?"

"Plausible? What do you mean?"

"Was she that kind of person?"

Anvers smiled. "Now you're using flattery. What would I know of suicidal types?"

"Okay. Just tell me what kind of person Mrs. Rooney was."

Anvers' eyes narrowed as he inhaled and then drifted to the window. "I liked her. Everyone who works here liked her. She was nice without being condescending. Some of the members feel guilty belonging to a country club and attempt to treat the employees as if we were all really on the same basis here. That won't wash. They don't wait on us, we wait on them. Nothing can change that. Mrs. Rooney was comfortable with the relationship and that made her easy to work for. And she really used the facilities of the club. She was a superb athlete."

Anvers was started now and Horvath just let him go. The manager needed no prompting. Clearly Mrs. Rooney had been a favorite of his. Maybe that's why he didn't mind talking. Whatever he had to say about Barbara Rooney counted as speaking well of the dead. The Barbara Rooney Mr. Anvers admired was a paragon of the virtues that make a good clubwoman. At least that was Cy Horvath's conclusion. She chaired committees, she won tournaments, organized dances.

"Angela Sykes is a member here too, isn't she?"

Anvers' eyes became hooded. He had lit a second cigarette and now stubbed it out in a tray. He shook his head. "That's enough, Lieutenant. I'm not going to waste the morning gossiping about the members."

"What have you got against Mrs. Sykes?"

"I have nothing against or for her. That would suggest I rank the membership here. That would be very presumptuous of me."

"Angela Sykes is quite a woman about town. In my line of work you learn those things. People rank themselves, Anvers. We just notice."

"That may be your job. It's not mine."

"I didn't see you at Mrs. Rooney's funeral."

"I was there."

"So was Mrs. Sykes."

"Was she? It could have been a better turnout."

"Maybe the members didn't like Barbara Rooney as well as the employees of the club did."

"They didn't."

"Why?"

"I don't know. Someone in my position may notice something like that, but members do not confide in me. I would not want them to."

"You must hear them talking."

"I try not to eavesdrop."

"How long have you worked here, Anvers?"

"Seven years. Not quite seven. I started in January."

"Are you the senior employee?"

"I suppose I am. Except for Georgie, of course."

"Who is Georgie?" Horvath asked.

9

EDDIE left his polishing machine to come down to tell him the cop was talking with Anvers. Eddie had been impressed by the man's size. And the look in his eyes.

"Steel, man. That's one cop you don't want to run into in the line of duty. He could whip the two of us with one hand, Georgie."

"A plainclothes cop?" Georgie was trying to remember if there had ever been a cop in the club before. Off-duty cops in the parking lot for big dances yes, but a cop asking questions of the manager? Georgie was pretty sure this was a first. He was also sure that he was here about Barbara Rooney.

Thank God. It couldn't have been suicide. Georgie would bet anything on that. Barbara Rooney had loved life. He repeated the thought, reassured by its unoriginality. It had the ring of an adage. It sure applied to Barbara Rooney.

"They in Anvers' office, Eddie?"

"No. At a table in the bar."

So Anvers was talking to him at least. You never knew with Anvers. Georgie could not understand fat men and Anvers was no exception. He was very haughty with the other employees. Well, it was a tough job, manager. Georgie had always thought so. Boss, but not a member; the manager could always be brought down to size by a member so what kind of authority did he have?

The only one to do the job with finesse had been Brooks and that had been years ago. Georgie wondered what Anvers would tell the cop. What had been the manager's conception of the dead woman?

"Thanks, Eddie. And I'm not here. I don't want to talk to no cop."

Georgie closed the door of the hideaway, watched Eddie amble off through the locker room, testing the doors as he went. In his lounge chair, Georgie tipped back and considered the ceiling. He had read a bit about meditation in a paperback he picked up in a drugstore, and he liked to think of the thinking he did here as a kind of meditation. It was funny how the rippled ceiling could assume different shapes and forms, suggest pictures and designs, as if it were a screen catching different projections. Georgie thought of the pictures on the ceiling as cast there by his subconscious mind, forms and shapes, if he could figure out what they were, they would tell him what was going on deep inside his mind. He hadn't read that in the book. It was his own theory, and he liked it.

That poem was not his only claim to fame. Not that he wanted anyone else to know about it either. That son of a bitch Olson had kept the original copy of the poem but Georgie had written it down before he could forget it. Forget it. There was no chance at all he would forget that poem, particularly after what had happened to Mrs. Rooney. At the cemetery, when they buried her, Georgie had stood there and said that poem in his mind. It was his way of saying good-by. He had cried. Nobody else had, at least he hadn't seen anyone else do it, but he had had to put his fist in his mouth to stop a sob from escaping. So, finally, the police were showing some interest in finding out who had killed her. No one could stop him from thinking of Mrs. Rooney now. Olson couldn't burst in on him and tell him to stop bothering Mrs. Rooney.

He hadn't seen much of Olson lately. Well, this was a slow season at the club. No. That wasn't it. Olson was in mourning for Barbara Rooney, Georgie was sure of it. The husband was taking it almost easily. Georgie admired him for contesting the verdict of suicide. Most members seemed to think Rooney was doing that just to be doing it, as if everyone knew it really was suicide, only you didn't want to admit it. Nothing would ever convince Georgie that she had killed herself. Someone had killed her. But who? Thank God the police were still looking into the matter. Georgie had expected to have them snooping around the club before now, but better late than never. Not that the Barbara Rooney other people talked about and whose death the police investigated seemed the same woman he could find in the light and shadows of the ceiling of his hideaway.

Voices outside caused Georgie to lift his head. He recognized Anvers' voice. Anvers! Had the manager ever been in the locker room before? Georgie got soundlessly out of his chair, pulled the drape and looked through the one-way mirror. Anvers was coming toward him followed by a man as big as Eddie had claimed the cop was. Cripes. Did Anvers know about his hideaway? Stupid question. Everyone knew about it now. Eddie, Olson, even Maggie Regan and now, apparently, Anvers. The fat bastard kept on coming and then there was a knock on the door. The big man leaned against the mirror, as they waited for Georgie to open up.

Georgie opened the door and came out before the cop knocked again and feigned surprise when he encountered Anvers and the cop in the locker room. "This is Georgie," Anvers said. His tone suggested that Horvath had been wrong to doubt him.

The cop looked impassively at Georgie and his eyes grew smaller.

"Don't you recognize me, Georgie?"

"Geez. You know, I do." Georgie, smiling, encircled the big man. There was something familiar about him, but what? "Don't tell me you used to work here?"

"We were caddies together. Horvath."

"Cyril! Sure, I remember you. For crying out loud, a cop."

"And you're still here."

It was just a statement, neither praise nor blame, but it set Georgie off. He babbled on about what a great job he had until even to himself he seemed to be apologizing for something. The trouble was it made him sound like someone who had never grown up, working here at the club the same way he had as a kid, where Horvath too had worked when he was a kid. Think of all the kids who had spent a summer or two at the caddy shack and then gone on to other things. Most of them probably didn't even remember working at the club. No doubt Horvath hadn't thought of him before he walked out the door of the hideaway.

"I'll leave you two," Anvers said, as if he had just arranged a big reunion. "I've got work to do upstairs."

"Someplace we can sit?" Horvath asked when Anvers had waddled away.

Georgie pointed to the benches there in the locker room.

"The manager said you had an office down here."

"An office! Come on. I've fixed up a little closet, that's all."

"Let's talk there."

Horvath headed toward the door Georgie had closed behind him tightly when he came into the locker room. There was nothing to do but let Horvath in.

It was a big mistake; Georgie knew that as soon as Horvath stood in the middle of the hideaway and gave the room a real onceover. He filled up the place, no doubt about that; if he stretched out his arms he could have touched the walls. And then he drew aside the drape and looked through the one-way mirror at the locker room. He let the drape fall back into place. Georgie waited but Horvath said nothing. He was ready to sit now.

"When he said Georgie, I was hoping it was you, the same one. You have been working here all these years?"

"I like it."

"That means you must know the members better than anyone else around here."

"I know them," Georgie said evenly. "It's my job."

"I know it is. So you keep tabs on them." He didn't even glance at the one-way mirror but they both knew what he was talking about. Georgie adjusted his chair and, sitting on the edge of it, looked at Horvath.

"Barbara Rooney, Georgie. Tell me about her."

"I don't know much that you won't already know, Cyril."

"Cy. Pretend I don't know anything."

The spiel that Georgie gave was true enough; it gave a fairly good picture of Mrs. Rooney. But Horvath's little eyes remained unblinkingly on him. Didn't he believe what he was being told? Georgie began to think that Horvath knew what he wasn't telling him, at least enough to know it was missing, and he was waiting for a fuller account.

"Was she faithful to her husband?"

"What kind of question is that?"

"One that can be given a yes or no answer."

"What did Anvers tell you?" Georgie could imagine that fat son of a bitch passing on all the gossip to the police, trying to create the impression that he was on intimate terms with the members. Well, Georgie knew what most of them thought of that slob.

"Answer the question, Georgie."

"How the hell would I know the answer to a question like that?"

"I don't know. Lots of ways. Not many secrets stay that way."

"She was a good woman, Horvath. A real lady. Whatever Anvers told you, forget it. People will say anything, that doesn't make it true. She wasn't like that."

"What was she like?"

It should have been easy to answer that question but Georgie felt incapable of even beginning to put Barbara Rooney into words. What would it mean to Horvath if he learned that she had been a great athlete, on the golf course, on the tennis courts. Her blond sun-streaked hair, the skin a little leathery from years of sun, her walk swift, almost floating, and her eyes.

They were gray and twinkly so that when she looked at you she gave the impression that you shared some secret. But that was still the public Barbara Rooney. How could he begin to say what the woman had been like to whom he had actually written a poem. Well, most of one. An awful thought occurred to Georgie. If Horvath talked to Dr. Olson, the dentist would give him that unfinished poem. Georgie blushed in anticipated shame. It was a preemptive strike when he told Horvath about Olson.

"He's her dentist?"

"That's not the point. He's a member here too. He stood up for her when guys talked about her in the locker room. It was just talk. Locker room talk, but they shouldn't have said those things about her. Olson told them that and they made fun of him." Horvath passed a hand over his face, cocked his head to one side and stared at Georgie.

"What exactly do you do here, Georgie?"

So Georgie kept right on talking. When had he talked to anyone like this? But it was a relief to get away from the topic of Barbara Rooney and away from Olson too. He made his job sound pretty interesting in the process.

"Then you're not married?"

"Me? I'm having too much fun."

That was a mistake. Horvath paused a moment before saying, "Tell me about Barbara Rooney and Dr. Olson."

Cyril got more comfortable, waiting for Georgie to go on. How the hell could he talk to Horvath and not really tell him anything? No wonder Anvers had been relieved to put the cop onto Georgie.

"I never knew you was a cop."

Cyril smiled. Oh, God. Georgie wished now the police had lost interest in Mrs. Rooney's death. If he told Horvath about Olson, the dentist would produce that poem. Georgie hated to think what Horvath would make of that poem.

"Olson is a dentist," he began. "I guess Mrs. Rooney was one of his patients."

10

THE ONE-STORY buff-brick building with a mansard roof and a parking lot that could accommodate over fifty cars was the center of Wanda's world. Here she managed the professional life of Martin Olson, D.D.S. Her title was clinic manager; new employees were instructed, by herself first and then by Dr. Olson, that for all practical purposes they were to take what she said as coming from the doctor himself. This went for the accountant, the receptionist, the dental technicians and the three other dental nurses. Wanda wore a pale green coat now, the same kind Dr. Olson wore, and that set her off from the others and seemed to confirm her authority. Patients often took her for a dentist and addressed her as Doctor. If someone else was present, Wanda corrected the misapprehension, otherwise not. The truth was that she felt capable now of doing anything Dr. Olson did. Not that she would attempt to operate, of course. But she could have done it.

She was like Olson too in the fact that her life was her work and vice versa. There was nothing outside the clinic that truly interested her. She came early and she stayed late. If she had any friend at all it was Florence Day, a surgical nurse at Fox River General. Flo found weekends almost as boring as Wanda did. They lived in the same building and used the indoor heated pool on both Saturdays and Sundays. They had met in the sauna. Can one nurse really tell another by sight? They both claimed later to have known right off that the other was a nurse. What was even clearer was that each was indisputable boss where she worked. They differed in that Flo despised doctors. She was unimpressed by Wanda's stories about Dr. Olson.

"So he makes a lot of money. A doctor or dentist would have to have two heads and no hands not to make money."

"He is the best oral surgeon in Fox River."

Wanda was irked that Flo took that as if it were on a par with the claim that he was the best mountain climber in the state of Illinois. Why should she try to impress Flo with Dr. Olson? It was enough that Flo was someone with whom she could talk more or less shop. It was true that Dr. Olson made tremendous amounts of money. Wanda knew. She saw the books. One Sunday afternoon some years before, Wanda went to the clinic and gave the books a good going over. The results were so impressive that she made periodic checks. Accountants came and went, so too business managers. Dr. Olson seemed to change them whenever he was about to make a good deal of money. The new person had no idea what a leap in income he had just enjoyed. But Wanda knew. Why did he want so much money? She herself was content with her salary, which was very good, and which got better when Olson realized that she represented continuity in his professional life. She had savings. She had a retirement fund. But she could never really imagine no longer working and, so long as she worked, what was so exciting about having money in the bank? The one thing she could not do was let Dr. Olson work on her teeth.

He did not understand this and it very nearly became a real bone of contention between them. When he accepted the fact that she could not be his patient, he used her as if she were his spy in the chairs of his rivals. She had gone to a variety of dentists over the past ten years, most of them picked by Dr. Olson, invariably men whose reputations were rising and who might have seemed to pose a distant threat to the prosperity and eminence of Martin Olson. Wanda learned to give him carefully modulated negative reports on the competition. He could not keep a smile from his lips when she reported defects in the technique of others. It seemed to bring them closer together. She might not mention it to Flo but she was perfectly honest about it with herself. Wanda intended to marry Martin Olson.

The match seemed an obvious one to her. She would go on working at the clinic, of course; that would remain their basic partnership. She had no romantic dreams about Martin Olson. She found him neither attractive nor repugnant, physically. He was someone she could understand. Someone with ambition. A man who put his nose to the grindstone and kept it there. He was shrewd about money in the manner of the self-made man. Whatever he had he had earned himself. She liked that. She refused to become his patient. She knew that being in the chair would make her seem just another vulnerable human being to him. Wanda knew that he looked on her as the iron maiden, unflappable, capable of handling any crisis. How could he be impressed with her under the light, mouth open, wincing at the touch of the drill? It had seemed axiomatic that he could never truly interest himself in a patient. Until Barbara Rooney came to the clinic, that is.

Wanda had known pain when her parents died in an automobile accident. She had known pain when a man she loved had spurned her. She had known her share of physical pain. But she had never before felt the kind of hurt that Dr. Olson's interest in Barbara Rooney gave her. The fact that he had tried to deceive her by saying Mr. Rooney insisted that he personally give her monthly checkups made it both better and worse. Wanda wanted desperately to believe this was true but she would have had to be a bigger fool than she was to do that. When Dr. Olson's interest in Mrs. Rooney became clear, Wanda had to find out as much about her as she could. Suddenly she had uses to which to put the time when she was not working — evenings, weekends. Barbara Rooney and her family became Wanda's obsession.

The location of the Rooney home had surprised her; a once fashionable neighborhood, it was now part of a triangle formed by highways and interstates. The house itself was a pleasant two-story brick structure set on an expanse of lawn. The driveway wound up the street to a three-stall garage. There were two Rooney children. Francis X. Rooney was a partner in the law firm started by his father. All in all, they seemed almost a parody of normalcy. And this was the woman with whom Martin Olson was helplessly in love. Wanda did not spare herself with euphemisms and false hopes. Martin Olson was in love with Barbara Rooney, or thought he was, and that was just as bad. She was a wife, the mother of two youngsters. She teased him and found him comic. That did not matter. There was only one solution so far as Wanda could see.

The thing had to be brought to fruition, become a fullfledged affair. With consummation would come a cure. Wanda talked the matter over with Flo, whose experience in such matters did not seem to be entirely second-hand. Flo asserted with wry wisdom that nothing makes a woman less attractive to a man than a night in bed. Oh, with the return of desire he will go through the motions again, but it is never really the same after. Flo considered the old ways best. All that should be saved for marriage. Wanda agreed. Though now, with the menace of Barbara Rooney, she would have done anything Dr. Olson asked of her. Anything. The trouble was that he simply did not notice her anymore. It was a sad thought that she had never existed for him as a woman, and she never would until he got Barbara Rooney out of his system. So let them go to bed together.

The problem was that Barbara Rooney turned out to be totally uninterested in Martin Olson. Whether consciously or not, she had been leading him on. She had teased him, flirted with him, and now, when he was completely taken by her, she treated him as though he were a clown. Wanda would have liked to take satisfaction in this outcome, but of course it only made matters worse. Now he would never be rid of her. Until he had her, Barbara Rooney would haunt his dreams and make Martin Olson inaccessible to Wanda. What to do?

The drama unfolded beyond her range. Dr. Olson spent more and more time at the Fox River Country Club. That was off limits to Wanda. Once Dr. Olson had taken her to a dance there. She felt she was involved in his effort to learn a foreign language. It infuriated her that he looked on the other members, the married members, as better than himself, in possession of some secret he did not know. She herself had been merely a prop, something he needed in the way he needed evening clothes. Throughout the night Wanda had known that she could have been replaced by any other woman and he would not have cared, if he even noticed. The evening did feed her fantasies about the life they would lead together, Martin and herself.

She had watched helplessly while his infatuation with Barbara Rooney grew even as it became increasingly unlikely that he would so much as hold her hand. But then Wanda's own loyalty to Dr. Olson increased. She was on the watch to see if any employees of the clinic showed awareness of what a fool Dr. Olson was making of himself. Apparently they had not even noticed. And then Barbara Rooney had been brutally killed.

At first, when there was the suggestion that it might be suicide, Wanda knew this was not true. Barbara Rooney had been killed. Martin Olson was told by a technician who had been listening to her radio rather than the Muzak that played endlessly in the clinic. One of their patients had been murdered or had killed herself; anyway, she was dead. Mrs. Rooney. Wanda had been with Dr. Olson at the time. He looked up and their eyes met. Her look was meant to be one of complicity, but he seemed not to notice her, to be looking right through her, to some horror impossible to describe.

11

THE PRESSROOM in the county-city building in downtown Fox River was not, as the name might suggest, a place of busyness and bustle, with intrepid reporters filing frenetic stories the better to insure an informed electorate. Indeed, a wag had once pinned under the door's legend another: While You Wait. The room did have a suggestion of weary romance about it. The desks were appropriately battered; there were scorched marks on their surfaces where untended cigarettes had burned themselves to extinction. There were chairs somewhat more comfortable than those at the desks scattered about, and against a wall there was a Naugahyde couch.

On that couch on this sunny October afternoon, Ninian slept, his sleep aided by the martinis he had begun to drink as accompaniments to his as yet unordered lunch and that ended by being lunch. Mervel, at a typewriter, was pecking away at something to which he darkly referred as "my novel." He had perhaps fifteen pages of this projected masterpiece in his possession, though he nursed the certitude that he had written and misplaced as many more. Today he wrote with the hope of a man who expects his plot and theme soon to appear. Mervel had read and believed that, in the course of writing imaginative fiction, there comes a moment when the writer hears an almost audible click. This signals that the story will from now on write itself. Mervel wrote, waiting in vain for that click. Gertrude Fingeret, literary and society editor for the *Fox River Shopper*, sat in a bar of sunshine, a cigarette in the corner of her mouth, knitting needles flying in her hands.

"Robertson has given Keegan more time to come up with a murderer of Barbara Rooney or he will have Phelps rule it a suicide."

"Says who?"

"Tuttle."

"Who got it from Peanuts." Gert took the cigarette from her mouth and coughed noisily for half a minute. On the couch, Ninian stirred and then subsided with a groan. Mervel's outstretched hands were poised over the keyboard of his typewriter.

The death of Barbara Rooney had promised much in the way of news, but so far it had been nothing but a disappointment. Whatever they might write here in the pressroom, editors were reluctant to print anything actionable about the wife of Francis X. Rooney. Rooney, Wirth, Hopkins, Barry and Rooney was a firm notorious for personal injury and libel awards that had set unnerving precedents both locally and nationally. It was a sign of the times that a violent death that had seemed a godsend now came down to rumors deriving from Peanuts and Tuttle. The former, a member of the locally notorious Pianone family, most of whose members fed at the public trough, had been taken onto the police force as part of some political deal no one retained clear memories of; perhaps because all participants were concerned to wipe it from their minds.

Tuttle's firm, Tuttle and Tuttle, consisted only of himself. The other Tuttle in the firm's title was his father who had helped

Tuttle *fils* through law school and had been granted titular immortality by his grateful son. It would not be too much to say that, were the local bar association to be asked to point out a member whose conduct and career exemplified the best in the ranks, Tuttle would not be chosen. He would fare no better if the request were for an example of a competent, unspectacular, average lawyer. Committees of the local bar had on several occasions heard complaints about Tuttle but as yet he had escaped censure, let alone disbarment. But that is how it was thought of: as yet. Tuttle had been the first lawyer in Fox River to avail himself of the opportunities presented by the relaxation of the rule against advertising. He had had a jingle recorded that was frequently played on various Chicago radio stations. "If you ever need a lawyer," it began, to the tune of the Marine Corps anthem. Thus far it had not paid to advertise — had not paid Tuttle, that is; the radio stations could not complain.

And there he was now in the doorway of the pressroom. He looked around, bright-eyed, tense, a bundle of energy, his Irish hat pulled low over his eyes. Surveying the room, he permitted himself to entertain the thought that, however rocky his practice had been over the years, up and down, up and down, his life was infinitely preferable to that led by reporters. Gertrude's brows lifted in acknowledgment of his presence, but she kept her eyes on her knitting.

The impulse that had brought Tuttle to the pressroom died. Let them find out for themselves the arrest that had just been made. Tuttle meant to show himself upstairs in the jail to see if the itinerant aluminum-siding man might want to hire counsel. As usual Tuttle had picked up the news from Peanuts.

Fredbo Hykley had been sought by the police ever since Barbara Rooney's body was found, if you could believe Robertson, which, Tuttle thought, you could if you did not mind running the risk of being deceived. Keegan had refused to comment on the arrest.

"Go ask Robertson."

Robertson would tell Tuttle or anyone else everything he knew, something quickly done. Apparently the chief regarded telling Tuttle and the handful of senior citizens who hung around city hall in the rheumy-eyed hope that scandal or fire or something would break out at any moment as the equivalent of a press conference. Tuttle had stopped by the pressroom to tell his friends of the Fourth Estate the news and suggest that they importune Robertson for a conference. The soporific scene that greeted his eye changed his mind. Ninian conked out on the couch, Gertrude with her knitting, Mervel typing, probably a letter home. Let these alleged reporters find their own stories. Tuttle had fish of his own to fry.

So he winked at the world at large and went back to the lobby where he took an elevator to the jail floor. He had a little trouble being admitted to see Fredbo, but by dropping the name Pianone several times, Tuttle gained admission to the cell block and there the visitors' table. At this hour of day there were no other visitors. Fredbo looked bewildered when he was led through the door and into the large room. The guard led him to the table across from Tuttle. The lawyer indicated that he should pick up the phone. When he had, Fredbo said, "Who the hell are you? I didn't order no lawyer."

"Every man has a right to legal representation," Tuttle said unctuously. But it was a right difficult to exercise without money.

"Free-lance aluminum-siding?" Tuttle mused. "Is there much money in that?"

Fredbo Hykley shrugged. "It depends. On the season, on the economy, on luck." Fredbo's hair looked brushed forward because his hairline was so low. His flesh had a boiled look about it and the small eyes did not inspire confidence. Tuttle pondered the man's remark. Fall could not be a good season for the siding business, the general economy was in a parlous condition, and Hykley did not strike him as a lucky man. Worse, he did not seem especially worried by the fact that he was locked up in the Fox River jail in connection with the death of one of its more prominent citizens.

"The court will appoint counsel for you, Hykley."

"You?"

Tuttle smiled. "Your court-appointed attorney needs the business. Tuttle doesn't."

"Who's Tuttle?"

Controlling his anger, Tuttle slipped Hykley his card.

"Taking into account good behavior, a lenient parole board, everything, my best case analysis is thirty-five to forty years. How old are you, Hykley?"

"Thirty-nine."

"Seventy-five, eighty when you get out. Well, who knows what strides science will have made by then. You might have a few good years left."

Hykley was shaking his head. "I didn't do it. I don't even know who the hell the woman is."

"Mrs. Barbara Rooney. She is a woman to whom you attempted to sell aluminum siding less than a month ago. And she lives in a brick house. There are witnesses who say you spoke to her in a threatening manner. Your truck was seen in the neighborhood several times after that. The fact that they arrested you when the chief was all but ready to let it go as a suicide looks bad for you, Hykley."

"But I didn't do it."

"Say that's true. The truth together with a good lawyer could make you a free man again."

"You want to be my lawyer, Tuttle?"

Tuttle smiled as royalty smiles at the peasantry. "I don't think you can afford me, Hykley."

"How much?"

"I don't think there's any point in getting into that. Is there?"

"Meaning do I have any dough? Don't worry. I can pay."

"Your notion of being able and mine could differ, Hykley."

Hykley slid forward on his chair and his shoulders lifted

as he leaned toward Tuttle. "I've got a bank account in Nashville." He looked around. In a whisper he said, "Seventeen thousand dollars."

"Do you have the passbook?"

"Don't you believe me?" Hykley sat back.

"Consider this a small lesson in legal procedure. From now on you will have to back up what you say with evidence."

Hykley said the passbook was in the stuff the police had confiscated from his pickup. Tuttle shook his hand, his own hand, indicating one of them stood for Hykley's. Tentatively, they were lawyer and client. Tuttle would check the passbook on his way out.

"They don't have a case, Fredbo. I'm surprised they arrested you."

"I thought I was going to get thirty-five to forty years."

"I meant life. And I meant with incompetent counsel. You are represented by Tuttle and Tuttle. I want you to get a good night's sleep."

"Have you ever been in jail?"

"Well, sleep as best you can. I shall spend the night planning our strategy."

He did not anticipate an onerous night. He truly was surprised by Hykley's arrest. That they might question the man made sense but they could not seriously believe that Hykley had murdered Barbara Rooney. What about the typed note?

"Can you type?" he asked Hykley.

"Don't you have a secretary?"

Witty or dumb, it was difficult to say. He asked Hykley where he had been on the Tuesday night or Wednesday morning that Barbara Rooney was killed.

"That's the problem. I was in the neighborhood where the woman was killed. The night before I was out drinking, you know, here and there, hitting the bars. I got lost when I tried to find my way back to my room. So I slept in the truck."

Tuttle did not like this. The story he had heard had not included this relevant particular. That damned Peanuts. When would he learn to tell important from unimportant things? Tuttle did not mind losing a case, he had lost his share, just so long as he went down to defeat with sure money in his pocket. It all hinged on that passbook. Well, it always had.

Hykley pushed away from the table and stood. Behind him, a cop moved away from the wall. "Only with two fingers," the prisoner said.

Tuttle stared at him, uncomprehending.

"Type. I make out my own bills and I type my checks too."

Tuttle nodded. Great. Hykley went away in the custody of the guard and Tuttle picked up his briefcase from the table. A thought crossed his mind. What if Fredbo Hykley had killed Barbara Rooney? Keegan would not have gone along with the arrest of Hykley if he thought there was no case against the man. Tuttle straightened his shoulders. Every man has a right to legal representation. And thank God for that savings account in Nashville.

12

Did Wanda know what he had done? Did she suspect he had killed Barbara Rooney? When the news flew through the clinic and their eyes met, it seemed to Martin Olson that his oldest and most trusted employee knew he was a murderer. Neither of them said a thing but it was as though they had entered into an agreement. Martin Olson realized that whatever Wanda suspected, he was not worried. The knowledge seemed as safe in her mind as in his own.

This realization came when he looked up and met Wanda's gaze. If the realization was sudden, what he realized had been there all along. And there was something else. For the first time he understood how silly he had appeared to Barbara.

Wanda looked at him with the same dogged devotion he had looked at Barbara. Why should someone who desires you be undesirable? Surely that could not be a law. If it were, marriage would be impossible. No, there were simply two instances of the same thing. Two similar but non-transitive relations. Wanda wanted Martin who wanted Barbara. There was no logic that could reverse the flow of that sequence.

From crossword puzzles, Martin Olson had turned to elementary logic books for recreation. He had a small computer in his apartment and spent hours at its console, lost in the fleeting abstractions on its green screen. It helped now to think of what had happened in abstract terms. That is how he planned the murder. Barbara was someone he could never have. This he had come to see. Nothing would change it. He had made a fool of himself with her. To redeem himself in his own eyes he had to provide a more acceptable ending of his pursuit of her. Simple failure and rejection would not do. If Barbara were dead, defeat would be acceptable. Only one involved in what has come to be called "health delivery services" knows how easily the aim can be reversed. Knowing how quickly a human being can bleed to death, Martin Olson could not bring himself to donate blood. His imagination, coupled with knowledge, made it impossible. The whirring machine that extracted a pint of blood could, if allowed to run but a few minutes more, drain the body. Olson was particularly careful about bleeding when he performed surgery. When he decided that Barbara Olson must die, the method suggested itself immediately. It would not do to use a method that suggested medical experience but it was his medical experience that told him how easily and quickly death could come when the veins are opened. He had no wish to be cruel to Barbara. Of course, killing her was cruel enough.

Did anyone other than Wanda suspect what he had done? He had expected to be questioned about the fact that he had had dinner, albeit an unscheduled one, with Barbara Rooney the night before she died. With Barbara and Angela Sykes. If he had been inclined to waver in his resolution, that meal with the two women would have strengthened him. Did they think he was unaware of their condescension? Their ruse to get rid of him was crude but he put up no resistance to it. But he followed them to the Gutter Ball; he sat in the gloom and watched them at the bar. He was not surprised when they picked up the two men and eventually took them back to Angie's. He nearly froze, waiting in his car. The temperature had dropped into the thirties. At four Barbara emerged. Following her to her house, it occurred to him that the men who had left Angela's shortly before Barbara could be suspected of the murder. That would not do. The plan was to have suspicions fall on her husband, Frank. It was as if he did not think Frank Rooney's colossal complacency could be disturbed simply by the death of Barbara. To be accused of it as well would be necessary. Hence the mystifying typed note, stuck in the carriage of a machine on which it had not been typed. Olson carefully wiped the keyboard of the typewriter in Frank Rooney's den after tapping out the note. And he had taken away the razor blade he had brought with him to cut her wrists. It was a risk to render the sleeping Barbara helpless with a shot of Novocain, but he did not want a struggle when he killed her. When he undressed her and lifted her over the side of the tub he felt no desire for her at all. If anything, her naked body was repellent. After cutting her wrists, deeply, firmly, his hand steady, he put them immediately under the lukewarm water with which he had filled the tub. Blood formed graceful shapes as it flowed from her wrists into the water. Martin Olson left the house with a sense of satisfaction. He had done what he decided to do. He had left behind a confusing and, he hoped, intriguing scene. It would be difficult for the police not to think of Frank Rooney as his wife's killer. Motive? The way she had spent the last night of her life was bound to come out, providing ample cause for jealousy and rage on Frank's part.

If he had done his work exactly according to plan, nothing afterward happened as he had imagined it would. In the first place, there was a surprising and irritating reluctance to accept the fact that Barbara Rooney had been murdered. Frank was furious at the suggestion of suicide and Martin Olson thought he could understand that, particularly when he considered the Catholic past of the Rooneys. The sin of despair, wasn't that the phrase for suicide? Despite everything Martin had done, the police leaned toward a verdict of suicide. And now they had arrested a Tennessee free-lance aluminum-siding man. It would have made more sense if they had rounded up the two men with whom Barbara and Angie had spent the fateful Tuesday night. Apparently they had not found out about them. It was an odd thought that people would keep quiet about something like that. Surely someone else at the Gutter Ball that night had seen Barbara and Angie leave with the two men. The police had been diverted onto the scent of Fredbo Hykley. Martin Olson was almost annoyed by this.

Then Olson detected relief in Wanda's manner and this irritated him too. It would have been a satisfaction to discuss what he had done with someone, and Wanda's constant presence in his professional life made her as likely a candidate as any, but of course this was out of the question. He could not discuss with anyone the fact he had murdered Barbara Rooney. The thought of doing so brought his first shiver of real apprehension. The arrest of Hykley showed the penalty the real world exacted for what he had done. He no longer felt that it would never in a million years occur to the police to suspect him. He was not worried about Wanda; he really wasn't. But there were others who might begin to put two and two together. It began to seem ominous that there was no mention in the paper of how the victim had spent the Tuesday night. Was Angie Sykes living in fear that it would come out how she and Barbara had spent the night? He imagined Angie being interrogated by the police. They would ask that she tell them all about the night with Barbara. How could she fail to mention that Dr. Martin Olson had joined them at their table? He would give anything now if only he had been more discreet. Angie would recall that night, she would remember Martin Olson and the police would be on his doorstep. What would be the right note to strike? He decided to be as matter-of-fact as possible. But Wanda had to be kept out of the imagined scene. She would say or do something whose results could be tragic. She could do him in by the very fact that she wanted to help him. Angela Sykes was another matter entirely. How easily he could imagine Angie blowing the whistle on him. She would form the image of him at dinner with her and Barbara. Olson imagined that Angie would be the first to point the finger at Martin Olson.

There was no need to phone her, knowing her habits as he did. The Gutter Ball was ideal for his purposes. He could get into and out of the place unnoticed and not even the waitress could identify him afterward with any conviction.

The fact that the police were only belatedly investigating the death made him feel, absurdly, that he had been concealing facts from them. The tremor of fear he felt at the thought of being caught had its own peculiar pleasure. He had killed Barbara Rooney and now must bet on the inability of the Fox River police department to follow the clues that were right before their eyes. When one knows what others do not, it is impossible to imagine that one could go undiscovered.

The eyes never really grew accustomed to the lack of light in the Gutter Ball and it took him some time before he got seated against the back wall of the bar room, a small table in front of him. The waitress who guided him to the free table, hand under his elbow, had a tray in her other hand and did not really pay much attention to him. She had an enormous beehive hairdo, enormous breasts, enormous hips: the extremities of the abbreviated costume she wore accenting her physical endowments; the hair was outrageous in its own right. Martin Olson ordered beer. He did not care for beer; he had never acquired a taste for drink of any kind. He had a pedant's knowledge of wine but no palate. If it would not have attracted attention to himself, he would have ordered a soft drink. But the Gutter Ball was a place where serious drinking was done. Ordering merely beer was risky enough. In any case, there would be a long delay before it arrived.

The bar of the Gutter Ball was three-quarters of a circle

and the room formed a kind of fan around it. There were perhaps a dozen stools at the bar — substantial, comfortable stools, with padded backs and armrests — and on the floor accommodations for what? Martin Olson guessed fifty to seventy-five people. He was wrong. The Gutter Ball had been approved by the Fire Department for one hundred and ten patrons at one time.

Business was good, but then business always seemed good at the Gutter Ball. The laughter, the voices, the hum in the room, suggested the daring and illicit. At the piano, bathed in a blue spotlight, a blonde in a green dress whispered golden oldies into the mike, every lyric suggestive as rendered by her. "I can't give you anything but love," she sang, her voice a moan, a bitch in heat, passion out of control. Martin Olson marveled that it was only a performance.

Those at the bar were silhouetted against the glow that arose from lights recessed in the bar area. Heads were close together, the laughter was more abandoned there, drinks were replenished more frequently. Angela Sykes, her fur tossed back over her stool, leaned into the light, a cigarette held before her in tapering, theatrical fingers. She was speaking rather earnestly to the man beside her; bald, he seemed not quite large enough for the stool in which he sat. Did his feet touch the floor?

Just so Martin had watched Barbara and Angela fall into conversation at the bar the last night of Barbara's life. Here, not yet a month later, was Angela, back at her post, apparently over whatever grief she had felt at the death of her companion on these nightly sprees. Was she a danger to him? An answer to the question was difficult to come by there in the Gutter Ball, the room filled with smoke, the smoldering voice of the vocalist, laughter. Why did the voices carry the note of despair? Martin had a sudden vision. What if the Gutter Ball were hell, or purgatory, some penitential place whose habitués were paying for their sins? He sat back, surprised by the idea. It was not in his usual line of thought, so much so that he doubted its originality. And then he remembered. It was a transposition of a thought of Barbara's. She had made the remark at a dance at the country club, looking around the festive room, the happy couples. Suddenly the whole aspect of the room changed. People who had previously seemed to be enjoying themselves now looked as if they were suffering torments, no matter the smiles on their faces.

"Sisyphus," Barbara mused. She looked at Martin and her eyes crinkled ironically. "I was such a good student at Rosary College, Martie. You wouldn't have recognized me. Anyway, that's our life, rolling a huge rock up a hill and just before we push it over the top it rolls down again and we have to do it over. And over." She smiled and her teeth looked white and perfect in her tanned face. Martin loved her teeth. "That was Sisyphus's punishment in hell."

That stayed in his mind, if not in his conscious mind. His brain cells were chock-full of images of her, of her words. Barbara was dead but she would always be with him in this way. Her remembered remark transformed the Gutter Ball. He found it easy to imagine that what people do for fun is the most painful activity of all. He had always found it that way. Wasn't this why he had had so much difficulty with Barbara? And with others. With Angela?

The man beside her bowed his head and Angie planted a big kiss on it. There was a burst of laughter and applause and the singer wavered and lost a note. The little bald man beamed at being the center of attention. He seemed very drunk. Angie threw an arm around his shoulders. It seemed a signal that he was indeed her companion for the night. Martin relaxed. Eventually his beer came and he drank it. Angie's laughter drifted through hell or purgatory. Where was Barbara now? Martin shook the thought away.

13

DURING as much of the daytime hours as she saw, Angie felt a mild contempt for the lives most people led. Routine, duty, living by the clock. It looked, and was, so dull. It was the kind of life Jerry not only led but praised. The day to day, the ordinary. "That is the poetry of life, Angel," he would say, his eyes moist with emotion.

"Then give me prose, sweetie."

"Whatever you want!" And he meant it. Such exchanges had usually ended with a trip, to Corfu, to Trinidad, to Singapore, someplace absolutely elsewhere. But with Jerry at her elbow it might as well have been home. What she really wanted was to get away from him. It had taken time to summon the courage to do it. But if she despised daytime people she had few illusions about those she met at night. Like Willie here, if that was his real name. They almost never gave their real names. Did they think she would want to blackmail them? Josephine asked Willie to bow again so she could see the imprint of Angie's lipstick on his bald pate. Whatever his name, Willie was a lot of fun.

Several rounds of drinks appeared before them on the bar, tokens of appreciation for the way she had decorated his head. Good. Angie liked to drink. So did Willie, but he obviously didn't hold it very well. He looked as though he would conk out before the night was through. She did not feel regret, she did not feel elation. *Qué sera, sera.* That was her motto. But Willie did look like someone who would be a lot of fun. Those little pudgy bald guys were often a real surprise. Well, time would tell. The night was still young so far as Angela was concerned. Bobby was singing Cole Porter now, "Night and Day," trying too hard, but not even she could ruin that one. The lyrics of popular songs were the only wisdom Angie knew and she nodded at the familiar words as believers respond to oft-repeated texts.

"I'm going to the john," Willie said in a stage whisper.

"Well, you'll have to go alone."

"Where is it?"

"Go past the piano and turn left." Willie got off his stool all right. He began to negotiate across the floor and without mishap until he neared the piano. Apparently tripping over someone's extended foot, he careened into the piano. Bobby was holding a note at the time, head thrown back, tremolo. When Willie stumbled into the piano, that instrument, being mounted on wheels, began to roll. Bobby's note became a scream as she was crushed back into the wall amid a general cascade of sheet music. The bowl filled with her tips hit the floor and rolled into the dark. The mike was still working. That is why, from under the tumble Willie and the singer made, could be heard quite distinctly Bobby's complaint, "You stupid son of a bitch." That struck everybody as funny. The Gutter Ball rocked with laughter. Willie was helped to his feet and the singer was all but ignored. The piano was rolled back into place, the microphone righted. And someone called, "Speech." The cry was taken up. "Let's hear from the stupid son of a bitch."

When Willie's amplified voice filled the Gutter Ball, it was pretty obvious he was drunk. He slurred words, he was incoherent. Everyone loved it. When Bobby got settled at the keyboard again, she got into the spirit of things and began to play a muted accompaniment to Willie's babble, humming along. Willie was a hit and Angie felt an absurd little pang of jealousy, as if she were losing him to fame.

Willie never did get to the john, not on that try anyway. After ten minutes of his nonsense, the mood changed and peanuts and lemon peels and wadded-up sodden bar napkins sailed through the air at Willie. One of the waitresses steered him back to the bar where he was greeted with yet more free drinks. God, it was fun. It was nearly two in the morning when Angie left the Gutter Ball. She had been trying to get away for half an hour, but Willie was not doing very well by then. There was a lengthy drunken reconciliation with Bobby when they passed the piano, actually a duet featuring the vocalist and Willie, so bad it was good. Finally they continued toward the door. But Willie had to stop at the men's room.

Angie waited for fifteen minutes and Willie did not appear. When she realized what she was doing, she stopped doing it. Willie must have fallen asleep in a stall. The prospect of sleep was overpoweringly attractive. Angie went out to where her car was parked in the lot, conscious that she was making an effort not to weave.

She was used to driving home in a less than sober condition. The trick was to pay very close attention to what she was doing. Often it helped to keep one eye closed. Somehow this improved her focus. Her car seemed almost to know the way home from the Gutter Ball. The route took her along the river road and then across the Stratton Bridge. She mustn't go too slowly. That attracted police as much as the failure to stay on the right side of the road. Twice Angela had been stopped in this condition, and twice she had been let off without a citation. In the first case, her name had been recognized and the patrol car escorted her home. The second time, the officers seemed to think something awaited them when they got her home, but she had bade them good night firmly, closed her door and locked it.

Tonight, as if to recall her to the intricacies of her task, she backed into a car as she maneuvered out of her parking place. It made an enormous bang. Angela shifted gears quickly and shot forward, out of the light, turning left in the direction of the river. Maybe it was because she was alone. Suddenly she was assailed by memories of Barbara Rooney and that final night they had spent together. God, how sad life was. All Barbara had wanted out of life was a little fun, and a little fun was all she got, really. Whoever got much more than a little? The thought that life was a bad joke was a familiar one. Angie preferred thinking of herself as the victim rather than the villain. So she had treated Jerry badly. She was just passing on what life had given her. In moods like this she could admit to herself that it really was not much fun to spend night after night in places like the Gutter Ball. The trouble was there were no alternatives that attracted her. That was what she meant by life's being unfair.

Tears formed in her eyes, a delicious lump of melancholy formed in her breast. At home, she would pour a brandy, put on a Roger Whittaker album, lie in bed and have a good cry. She would think of Barbara. God, how sad.

As she drove along the river road she had the eerie feeling that she was not alone. She imagined that Barbara Rooney was in the passenger seat. The ghost of Barbara Rooney? That didn't sound absurd. There was another presence in the car. Angie's grip on the wheel tightened but she did not feel fear. She said in a whisper, pronouncing each syllable distinctly, "Barbara?"

Did she expect an answer? She repeated the name of her dead friend, more demandingly now.

"Barbara, say something."

The sound behind her, although it seemed to come in response to her summons, startled her. First there was the reflection in the rear-view mirror. Then Angie turned and looked wildly over her shoulder. Martin Olson sat in the back seat, a terrifying expression on his face. In his lifted hand was a hypodermic needle. Screaming, Angie lost control of the car, which bumped over the curb and headed erratically toward the river.

14

Roger Dowling heard it on the radio while he ate his breakfast, Marie Murkin brought him periodic updates throughout the day, but the story was far from clear. A car had gone into the river last night and the woman in it had been drowned. Marie nodded as she spoke of it, the movement of her head seeming to put her into synchronization with some cosmic explanation Roger Dowling did not begin to fathom. Marie Murkin was old enough to accept women's intuition as the name for what she had.

"It's foul play, Father, mark my words. People don't just drive into the river and drown."

"Wasn't she alone in the car?"

Marie Murkin smiled as women have smiled since Chappaquiddick. It was a relief when Phil Keegan came over that evening and Roger Dowling got a non-intuitive account of what happened to Mrs. Angela Sykes. By that time the pastor of St. Hilary was not without curiosity. An arrest had been made. A man named Virgil Rushton. Marie's smile was triumphant but, to her credit, she said nothing. After she served Phil his beer she left the study, nor did she stop halfway down the hall to overhear Captain Keegan's account.

"Why did you arrest Virgil Rushton, Phil?"

"They were seen together earlier. At a dive called the Gutter Ball. They left together."

"People saw the woman leave with Virgil Rushton?"

"Everybody in the bar calls him Willie, but it's the same guy."

"Was the woman sober when she died?"

"She was sloshed."

"So why can't it be an accident? Maybe your Virgil Rushton just got out of the car when he could and she drove into the river and drowned."

"Then he should have reported it. Not that he was in any condition to."

"Where did he spend the night?"

"Well, we arrested him in his room at the Slumbertown Motel."

"That's pretty far from where the car and body were found, isn't it?"

"Somehow he got back to the Gutter Ball. He took a cab from there almost an hour after he had been seen leaving with Angela Sykes. Even drunk he could have walked back to the bar from the river in that time."

Roger Dowling had seen Phil Keegan like this before: Phil had a plausible explanation of what had happened and he didn't believe a word of it. And no wonder. Phil went on.

"The prints made by the man who got out of Angela's car before it continued into the river don't match Virgil Rushton's. Not a single fingerprint of his can be found in the car. I think we're going to have to let him go in the morning."

"He denies going with her in the car?"

"Roger, he doesn't remember a thing. He might have had amnesia. Imagine someone wandering around that drunk."

"Who do you think the man with her was?"

But Phil might not have heard the question. He exhaled cigar smoke in a thin steady stream. When he spoke, his voice had dropped. "The damndest thing, Roger. Barbara Rooney and the Sykes woman knew each other. They had been seen together, out on the town." Phil looked at Roger Dowling. "They were seen together the night before Barbara Rooney was killed."

"With the Rooney children?"

"Ha."

"But the father was in Wisconsin. Who was watching the children?"

"She dropped them off at the baby sitter's. That's why they weren't around when their mother died."

"I thought baby sitters came to the home of the children."

"Well, this is an aunt, not just a baby sitter. There was a standing invitation for Mrs. Rooney to leave the kids with her sister-in-law Nancy. She lives in the house her parents bought when they turned their home over to Frank and his family. Since Barbara played in tournaments so often, she needed someone to watch the kids. It got to the point where Nancy didn't even ask what the reason was. She didn't ask why the kids were being dropped off on that last night of Barbara's life."

"But why on earth didn't she tell you her sister-in-law had left the children with her the night before she died?"

"She didn't. That's all. And we didn't show enough curiosity to wonder about it." Keegan poured what remained of his beer into the glass and tossed it off.

"Don't blame yourself, Phil. Remember, you were battling Robertson. How did you find out about the dinner the two women had?"

"A dentist named Olson reported it. The women had asked

that he join them when he ran into them at the restaurant. He did but they parted there, the women going off without him. He feels awful for not having told us earlier. He assumed we knew at first, then began to wonder. He had expected to be asked about it and then when Mrs. Sykes was found drowned in her automobile in the Fox River, he came to us."

"They went off after dinner without the dentist? What did you say his name is?"

"Olson. Martin Olson."

"Where did they go?"

"Let me get another beer first."

Phil lumbered off to the kitchen and was soon back with another bottle. He sank back into his chair. "Where did they go? They went to the Gutter Ball."

"Aha."

"Cy finally managed to pry this out of the bartender there, the nighttime bartender, a woman named Josephine. He had one of his hunches and pursued it and, sure enough, the Gutter Ball is where those women went after they left Olson. Josephine regrets telling Cy that but it's too late now. He will stick with her until she remembers something about the last night of Barbara Rooney's life if he does nothing else this year."

Roger Dowling was not surprised. Two women, acquaintances and more, friends who went out together, had spent their last nights on earth in the same bar.

"Did Frank Rooney know Angela Sykes very well?"

"He denies that his wife did. But he also denies that she was ever in a place like the Gutter Ball and there is no doubt she was there and more than once. The Sykes woman had a bit of a reputation for catting about."

"I suppose a wife could have a friend her husband knew nothing of."

"She could. Apparently the two women went out when Rooney was not in town. But Rooney knew her too."

Roger Dowling waited. There had been an uncustomarily dramatic tone in Phil's voice. Sipping beer now, he peered over the rim of his glass at Roger Dowling as if to see whether the significance of the moment was realized. He put down the glass.

"The footprints by Angela Sykes' car, where it stopped before continuing into the river, were made by Frank Rooney."

"He bailed out before the car plunged into the river?"

"Bail out isn't quite right. The car definitely came to a halt there. It looks as if she let him out before driving into the river." Silence fell in the rectory study. Smoke from Roger Dowling's pipe rose in thoughtful clouds as he tried to visualize the scene Phil conjured up. It was very difficult to make into a credible sequence. He could imagine a panicked passenger jumping from a vehicle that was headed for the river. He could imagine a suicidal driver shoving a passenger from a car before heading into the river. But the notion that the driver would come to a stop, that a passenger would step out, and then what? Stand there and watch the car go over?

"Did Frank Rooney report the car in the river?"

Phil shook his head.

"What explanation does he give of his footprints?"

"None. His sister Nancy suggests that the shoes were part of clothing she donated to St. Vincent de Paul when she got rid of Barbara's things. We're checking that out but it doesn't seem likely. She doesn't remember any other clothes of Frank's that went out with Barbara's."

"Was Frank Rooney seen with the Sykes woman that night?"

"Not at the Gutter Ball."

"Is there any sign he was inside the car, Phil? Can fingerprints be checked after it's been under water?"

Phil shook his head. "All we have are the prints of his shoes near the river. That's plenty."

"For what? At most it makes him a witness of a suicide. You can't prosecute him for not stopping her from driving into the river, can you?"

Phil Keegan waved this away with his still unlit cigar. He seldom lit a cigar until he had drunk two bottles of beer. "It's the connection with Barbara Rooney's death that interests me, Roger. A month after Barbara Rooney is murdered, the woman she had dinner with the last night of her life is found drowned in the river. The footprints of the murdered woman's husband are found at the scene, suggesting that he was in the car before it went over but was conveniently allowed to get out before it was too late. And Frank Rooney denies having been there by the river, his sister comes up with some far-fetched explanation of how his prints were found there, and Rooney refuses to sit down and discuss the whole matter with us. He says we have had more than enough time to catch the stranger who murdered his wife. At least his complaining has convinced Robertson we can have all the time we need on this. Rooney is threatening to hire a detective." Phil smiled wickedly. "I have sent Peanuts to Rooney to suggest that Tuttle would be a more plausible employee."

"Wouldn't Rooney know Tuttle?"

"Sure. But honest lawyers harbor the suspicion that guys like Tuttle can get things done in ways they would rather not know too much of. I'm counting on Rooney's being like that. Tuttle is a pain in the neck, but a private investigator would be a lot worse." Phil Keegan seemed to be reviewing all the instances when private detectives had made life more trying for him and the Fox River police.

"What could Frank Rooney tell you that you don't already know?"

Phil didn't have specific questions in mind. What he lacked was much of a feel for the kind of person Barbara Rooney had been and the kind of life she had led. There were certainly indications that her life was considerably different from what one might have thought. Her athletic prowess was widely known, of course, and with it her prominence in the activities of the Fox River Country Club. But the apparent habit of drinking evenings in the company of someone like Angela Sykes was a surprise. Sure, Angela was a member of the club too. At least her former husband was and while they were married she had been as prominent as Barbara Rooney in its activities. Its social activities; Angela was no athlete. Phil Keegan was used to surprises as a cop; most citizens were not quite what they seemed to be—well, many citizens. Respectable men sometimes were found in the most embarrassing places when police arrived on the scene. Husbands kept mistresses; women were unfaithful to their husbands—and to their lovers. Keegan knew all that. But the Barbara Rooney case was different. Barbara Rooney had two kids and she had been raised a Catholic.

"Apparently she didn't practice her religion, Phil."

"Her husband asked you to bless her grave."

Phil Keegan spoke as a man who lived what he believed. If, as the Baltimore Catechism told him, he had been created to know, love, and serve God in this life, and to be happy with Him forever in the next, that ought to have its impact on how he did live. And, in Phil's case, it did. He was a good man. Not perfect, certainly, but he could not believe that Barbara Rooney had been able to dismiss from her mind the great and simple truths of her religious formation. Well, that was Roger Dowling's area and he could believe it. Loss of faith is not necessary for people to set aside, apparently completely, their moral and religious professions when they act. The marvel, he had come to see, is that there are some who remain true to their ideals.

"So where do things stand now, Phil?"

"Cy is going to have a talk with Nancy Rooney. He thinks he detects something less than total devotion to her sister-in-law."

"Yes. That could be a promising avenue. I imagine he will want to have a session with the bartender too. Josephine, wasn't it? Her and waitresses, if there are any. If Frank Rooney was there with Angela, or there when she was, or simply lurking around, someone must have seen him."

After Phil Keegan left, Roger Dowling finished reading his office for the day and then decided against going upstairs immediately. He half-filled his pipe and touched a match to it. What Phil Keegan lacked, what must be bothering him and Cy and whoever else was working on this, was any overall story into which the events could be fitted and thereby take on meaning. Roger knew that Phil professed to distrust theories. Theories in the wrong sense of the term had a way of generating facts rather than accounting for them. Well, in the abstract, there might be a problem there. Roger Dowling's angle of vision was different, in any case.

Imagine Fox River, Illinois, as an infinitesimal section of a planet peopled by creatures whose lives have an eternal significance. It is a race, a test, a time of trial. As long as a human is alive, he can turn his mind to the destiny that is his and a loving God brooding over the world, inviting the free acceptance of his call, not able to force that free acceptance. This is the essential drama of human life, the drama that has informed the great literature of the West. Roger Dowling had a penchant for the medievals; the *Summa* of Aquinas and Dante's *Commedia* were constant companions. But the point could be made with Shakespeare, Milton, and Donne. The artist might try to capture the drama, but he can give only a foreshortened version of it. He can know the hearts of his characters, but no man can read the heart of another. And it is in human hearts that the drama essentially takes place. Keegan and Horvath had to deal in externals, the realm of justice. Roger Dowling's interest was the inward, the realm where mercy and forgiveness can penetrate. As a priest he hoped to be a means God used to dispense His mercy.

Thus, thinking of the brutally murdered Barbara Rooney,

of her husband, sister-in-law, her children, and thinking now as well of the sad drunken death of Angela Sykes, he took Phil's hint of a link between the two events. Imagine that someone caused both deaths. A first demand would be that the culprit be caught and punished. But what had driven a human being, a creature destined for eternal happiness, to do such deeds? Roger Dowling thought that one of the most horrendous scenes in Shakespeare was that in which Hamlet does not kill his uncle because he finds him at prayer. The thought that his enemy should go repentant into the next world stays Hamlet's hand. His revenge seeks an eternal punishment. Had the person who killed Barbara Rooney and Angela Sykes — presuming they had both been killed, presuming they had been killed by the same person — even thought of whether they were ready to move out of time into eternity?

It was the condition of that person's soul that now interested Roger Dowling. God was in pursuit of him, no matter that his hands were red with blood, that he bore the mark of Cain. God pursued him, not with an eye to punishment, but in order to forgive and reconcile.

His pipe seemed to have gone out. He tamped its contents and quickly withdrew his finger. The slightest burn, the smudge of ashes on his finger. It seemed to invite meditation on the Last Things. Roger Dowling smiled. The hour invited him to go up to bed and get some sleep.

He checked the doors of the rectory before going up. This was as much a concession to Marie Murkin as anything else. After checking the kitchen door, he looked across the lawn to the great shadow of St. Hilary's church. It too was locked. This seemed worse than locking the rectory, as if people must be kept from visiting God. But there were valuable things there, sacred things that thieves might steal. An odd world. A vale of tears. Roger Dowling turned and went down the hall to the stairs which led to his portion of the upstairs.

15

WHAT THE hell was going on, that's what Georgie wanted to know. He had been relieved when the police began to show some serious interest in the death of Barbara Rooney. It had been kind of fun to see old Cyril Horvath again. It was something, Horvath remembering him before he could remember Horvath. Maybe that was why Horvath was the cop and Georgie was assistant to the pro at the country club.

Fairwell had phoned from Sarasota this morning and they wasted a couple of minutes establishing that there was an hour's difference in the time between Florida and Illinois. Georgie told the pro everything was fine, nothing much happening, go ahead and enjoy your vacation. Fairwell hadn't liked to have his stay in Florida referred to as a vacation. He still dreamed of having at least a season on the tour and Georgie knew he was trying to qualify for a minor tournament that was meant to be the first step on the long road upward to fortune and fame. He told Fairwell about Angela Sykes.

"Jesus. That's too bad. How's Mr. Sykes taking it?" Georgie didn't know. The pro should be concerned about Gerald Sykes. He had given so many sets of lessons to the uncoordinated Sykes that he had actually cut his fee. Not that Sykes couldn't afford the lessons, and not that Fairwell had anything against money. But it began to seem a commentary on his ability to help members improve their games. So he gave Sykes what he called "refresher" lessons.

"Georgie, do me a favor. Go see Sykes, see how he's doing, then call me back. I don't want to phone him if he doesn't want people bothering him now."

"If he doesn't want people bothering him he won't want to see me."

"That's what I mean. Find out."

"You could send him a wire."

"Right. I will. I most definitely will do that, Georgie. But I'd like to telephone too, if that seems indicated. Angie Sykes, Jesus."

And then Georgie remembered. It was the biggest no-no of them all in a club like this: No hanky-panky between the help and the members. That most definitely included the pro. Well, there was some reason to think this was a rule Fairwell had bent if he hadn't broken with Angela Sykes. If anyone knew about it beside himself, Georgie would be surprised. Nor did he blame the pro. Angie was pretty notorious before the divorce, and since...well, Georgie had heard the stories. If she did hang around the Gutter Ball, that said it all. The Gutter Ball was where you went alone and did not leave alone. It was just a place of legend to Georgie. He had never been there. It was no place he wanted to go. Eddie knew a woman who had waited on tables there.

"Picture this big room, shaped like this." Eddie fanned out both hands, a wondering expression on his face. "Here is the bar, here are all the tables. The piano? Right here. And, Georgie, that room is dark. You cannot see your fist before your face." Eddie had closed his eyes to emphasis the point. "Now Julia tells me you got to watch where you're stepping when you walk through that room. I mean, things are going on there." Eddie's grin was wide and he shook his head slightly from side to side, eyes still closed. Georgie acted as if he were equally impressed but he found the bar disgusting. The trouble was he had no difficulty imagining Mrs. Sykes in such a place.

"She goes there. Julia seen her there more than once or twice. Her and Mrs. Rooney."

"Bullshit," Georgie said.

Eddie's eyes popped open. He looked shocked, then sly. "I forgot, Georgie. Scuse me. Your lady love. Maybe Julia was mistaken about her."

Georgie got away from Eddie as quickly as he could. If there was one thing Georgie could not bear it was being teased. When the Sykeses divorced they had sold the house across the county road from the entrance to the country club and moved into separate apartments. Mrs. Sykes had gone into a condominium near the river, Mr. Sykes had taken a little efficiency in a building in downtown Fox River, not far from the men's clothing store that was the source of his wealth.

Anvers maintained that the store was simply the supplier of capital for the investments that were the true source of the Sykes wealth. Whatever the explanation of it, Sykes had money and it didn't seem right that he should be living where he was. In the foyer, Georgie looked at the bank of buttons identified by apartment number alone. The only thing he was sure of was that Sykes lived on the second floor. He pressed 2A. A moment later a metallic voice, male or female, he could not tell, squawked in the earphone Georgie had unhooked and pressed to his ear.

"Mr. Sykes?"

"Sykes is 2D," the voice said testily.

Georgie went upstairs. Some security. Anyone could come

in off the streets and roam the corridors of the building. There was a peephole inset in the door of 2D and, after knocking, Georgie stepped back so that Mr. Sykes could get a good look at him. He felt as if he were getting his picture taken. Down the hall, a door opened and a very short woman with a head of hair like steel wool glared at him. She disappeared, pulling her door shut with a bang. 2A? 2D did not open. Georgie knocked again, half expecting to bring Mrs. Brillo out again, like the Storm figure on a clock. It took another knock before there was a muffled voice on the other side of the door. It was Mr. Sykes telling Georgie to go away.

"I'd like to talk with you, Mr. Sykes. This is Georgie."

"I can see, Georgie. Not today. Something terrible has happened."

"I know. That's why I'm here. Let me in, Mr. Sykes."

A long silence. Georgie was thinking of going away or knocking again, maybe contacting Anvers and letting him take responsibility. But then the door opened a few inches and the unshaven face of Mr. Sykes looked at him over a flimsy security chain, tears in his eyes.

"Please, Georgie. Go. I'm in no mood. Some other time."

"Fairwell phoned from Sarasota. I promised him I'd come see you."

"He's in Sarasota?"

Georgie nodded.

"Mrs. Sykes and I spent some weeks there once, maybe ten years ago." The memory brought fresh tears to his eyes. Georgie could see that Sykes was wearing a bathrobe, silk, but he seemed to be dressed.

"Let me in, Mr. Sykes."

Sykes shrugged, pushed the door closed and undid the chain. When the door swung open, Sykes was shuffling away. Georgie went in and closed the door, leaving the chain dangling. Now that he was in, he almost wished Sykes had refused to admit him.

† 103 †

What could he say that would console him? Sykes sat in the middle of the couch, legs apart, hands dangling between his knees. The light from the windows fell upon him and he looked older and grayer than Georgie remembered him. On the coffee table in front of him was a medicine bottle. Sykes looked from it to Georgie.

"Saved by the bell. I was about to take all those sleeping pills and call it a day. I'll take your timely arrival as a sign I shouldn't. My wife — my ex-wife — is dead."

"I heard."

Sykes nodded. "It's another news item, isn't it? Woman found drowned in car in river." Sykes had tried to make it a joke, but his voice broke and a sob escaped him. He put a hand over his mouth and looked abjectly at Georgie. Georgie was wishing Fairwell had not telephoned him from Sarasota.

He sat down across from Sykes, ignoring the crying. Why weren't Sykes's friends here with him now? It was an awful thought that he and Fairwell were the only friends Sykes had. How could they be friends? They worked at the club.

"Angela dead." Sykes shook his head.

"Was it an accident, Mr. Sykes?"

The question drew an angry look. "Of course not. And it wasn't suicide either. She was killed, Georgie. Killed the way Barbara Rooney was."

"But who did it?"

"Who did it?" Sykes smashed his cigar in an ashtray, bringing it down again and again. "I did. I killed her, Georgie." But the fire died in him as it had in the cigar. "With a kiss, Georgie. The coward does it with a kiss."

Georgie didn't know what to say to that. But then there didn't seem to be a need to say anything. Mr. Sykes was crying again. Georgie felt like crying himself.

"There are lots of ways of killing someone, Georgie."

"You were good to her, Mr. Sykes. Everyone saw that. People talked about it."

"Did they?"

"I noticed it myself."

Sykes's pleased expression faded. "Maybe I was too good to her. Maybe that was my fault." And Sykes was off again, in search of an imaginary guilt that could provide him consolation in his hour of grief.

16

THE PROSPECT before him made Horvath think it was Ladies Day. First he would talk with Nancy Rooney, then he would go on to the Gutter Ball and check out the story Josephine the bartender had given to Agnes Lamb. Agnes was black and a woman and only recently assigned to the investigative arm. Keegan still claimed to be skeptical about her. Cy thought she was good. She was also sensitive and he assured her that he was checking at the Gutter Ball as a matter of routine and not because he doubted the value of her report. "It's not a criticism, Agnes."

"Well, when you come to that, I'm not satisfied with that interview, Lieutenant." He had told her to call him Cy but she wouldn't do it. "That woman told me nothing and I knew she was holding back. I'll be interested to see what you get out of her."

Agnes had adopted the departmental prejudice that women talked to Cyril Horvath when they would talk to no one else.

There was some truth in it, but Cy didn't like too much made of it, because he didn't know what the reason for it was. And it wasn't just women. People talked to him. He found that the more silent he was, the more talkative people became. Keegan said it was his expression.

"In the singular. You've only got one. People can't read it and they talk to try to change it."

Nancy Rooney lived in a new development on the river north of town, the houses placed on oversized lots whose trees had been preserved during construction. This made the area seem more established than it was. The Rooney house was a large L-shaped ranch whose lawn now lay under freshly fallen leaves. Two kids had made a pile of leaves and were tumbling about it. The woman standing in the driveway, wearing slacks and an open corduroy coat, her hair pulled back in a ponytail, was Nancy Rooney. She turned when Horvath pulled into the driveway and stopped. Her squinty smile suggested she was nearsighted and couldn't yet see who he was. Horvath had spoken to her once before and his supposed magic with women had not seemed operative at the time. His guess about her eyesight seemed confirmed when her smile faded and a disapproving vee formed between her brows. She turned and looked across the yard at her nephews. Horvath identified himself.

"I remember you, Lieutenant."

"I'd like to ask you a few questions." She turned to him. Whatever their defect, her eyes were an attractive green. There were several threads of gray in her hair. Signs of age in an unmarried woman seem particularly sad.

"A few questions," she repeated.

"Could we go inside?"

"I am watching the children."

"I don't think they'll run away."

"Do you have children of your own, Lieutenant?"

He was saved from answering by the appearance of Frank Rooney. The front door opened and there he was. He let the door slam behind him and came striding toward his sister and Horvath, an angry look on his face.

"I don't want you talking to him, Nancy. If he hasn't told you, he is from the police. After the asinine things they've said to me, I don't think there is any point in cooperating with their ridiculous investigations."

Nancy Rooney bristled. Obviously she did not like anyone telling her what to do.

"You mean we can leave things in the competent hands of that idiot Tuttle?"

"Nancy, the police as much as accused me of drowning the Sykes woman. I suppose they think I killed Barbara too."

"They found your shoe print there, Frank. Would you expect them to ignore a thing like that?"

"Good God, do you think I did it?"

Horvath caught the whiff of whiskey on Rooney's breath. Nancy Rooney's expression suggested that she had a difficult house guest in her brother.

"No, Frank," she said with that patience adults reserve for children. "I don't think you've been killing people. Now I am going to talk with Lieutenant Horvath for a few minutes. Why don't you keep an eye on the boys?"

"They'll be all right."

Rooney turned and went back to the house. Nancy Rooney glanced at Horvath. "He's been drinking." Horvath said nothing. "Maybe I'd take to morning drinking myself if someone accused me of murder."

"No one has accused your brother of murder."

"How do you explain the footprints?"

"If you gave the shoes to St. Vincent de Paul, any number of explanations are possible."

"You sound skeptical about that donation."

Horvath looked up the drive toward the house. She took

the hint. "All right. Come inside. I suppose I have to cooperate or you'll lock up Frank. Not that that seems a very strong motive this morning."

The interior of the house was more expansive than the exterior suggested. The rooms were huge and opened on large windows not visible from the front. Horvath had the impression of being ankle deep in carpet as they crossed the living room. Nancy Rooney led him into an adjacent room that looked out on a wooded area. Horvath did not get the sense there were other houses nearby. She showed him to a leather, brass-studded chair. Seating herself across from him, still wearing her corduroy coat, she sighed. "All right, start the grilling."

"Tell me about Barbara Rooney."

The question half surprised her. She smiled. "Well, I suppose that is the heart of the matter."

She took a package of cigarettes from the pocket of her coat. He did not offer to light it for her. "I'll begin by saying that I didn't really care for Barbara." She brought the match she had struck to her cigarette and blew out the flame with exhaled smoke. "I didn't like her from the beginning. And don't think this was the usual thing, no one is good enough for my brother. I have few illusions about Frank. But I was surprised that he married someone like Barbara." Horvath waited and she went on. What had surprised her in her brother's choice of a wife was that Barbara was athletic. What used to be called a tomboy. Her brother on the other hand was only fair to middling at sports. Much too impatient to improve himself. She didn't know how Barbara could bear to golf with him. She always beat him.

"Did he mind?" Horvath asked.

"That depended. If he was preoccupied with something else, defeat in golf fell into perspective. Then it was just a silly game, hitting a ball around with a stick. But there were days when he took it seriously and then he was an extremely bad loser. One thing I'll say for Barbara. She never trimmed her game to let him beat her. She played only one way, the best she could."

"What didn't you like about her?"

"Well, you must have found that out by now." She waited but Horvath said nothing. "She ran around, Lieutenant. She saw other men. She went about with Angela Sykes to disreputable places where they picked up men like a pair of trollops."

"Your brother told you this?"

"I told him, Lieutenant. He will probably never forgive me."

"And how did you find out?"

Her chin lifted and she looked at him coolly as she considered her answer. "It was common knowledge."

"You just heard people talking?"

"Something like that."

"And told your brother what people were saying?"

"I saw her," she said sharply. The picture of herself as a purveyor of secondhand news did not appeal to Nancy Rooney.

"Tell me about it."

"Is that really necessary, Lieutenant? I am right in assuming that none of this is news to you, am I not?"

"I'd like to hear how you found out it was true."

"At the time I was not the least suspicious. It came as a complete shock. I belong to a bridge group." She did not say it, but Horvath got the impression that the other members of the group, like Nancy, were unmarried. Someone had heard of the Gutter Ball and they talked about it. The suggestion was made that they visit the place.

"It was meant as a joke, of course, but the idea grew on us, particularly when it appeared that one could look and not be seen because it is so dimly lit. So one night several of us went. We sat at a table and ordered a drink and I saw Barbara at the bar. With a man. A stranger. There was no possible doubt but that they were together. Fortunately the friends I was with did not recognize her. We did not stay for our drink. I wanted to get out of there."

"You told your brother what you had seen?"

"I went to Barbara first."

"What did she say?"

A touch of red appeared on Nancy Rooney's cheeks and she looked briefly away. "Among other things, she said she didn't expect me to understand. I told her I understood perfectly well. I told her what I thought of her. It was a heated exchange."

"And then you told your brother?"

"No. Despite the argument, I hoped that my talking to her would frighten Barbara into behaving herself. I suggested she seek counsel from a priest and though she scorned the suggestion when I made it, I hoped she would act on it. That was a forlorn hope. My brother and his wife had ceased the practice of their religion. When it became clear that Barbara had not changed her ways, I went to Frank. She seemed to be taunting me to do so. If she were afraid of his learning, of my telling him, she would have stopped. She did not. I talked with Frank."

"Who resented it."

"And would not believe me. I am not sure that he ever did."

"Yet it was widely known?"

"Widely enough so that he should have heard it from sources other than myself."

"What would he have done if he believed you?"

"Yes, I've thought of that. When I first heard the awful news about Barbara, the thought came that Frank had found out at last and had killed her. But even as I thought it I did not really believe him capable of it. It was far more likely to be one of her men, the people she took up with when she was on the town. And now poor Angela Sykes's death makes that a stronger possibility, doesn't it?"

"You think the deaths are connected?"

"Oh, come on, Lieutenant. Don't treat me as if I were an

ass. I admit I am in a disadvantageous position in this conversation, rather like a penitent and her confessor. But I am not stupid. Of course those deaths are connected. Would you be here if they weren't?

"Let me make a little confession, now that I've invoked the analogy. Those shoes of Frank's. I hadn't given them away. But he is certain they have been missing from his closet. The explanation seems obvious. Whoever killed Barbara took those shoes along. Her death, I mean Barbara's, was made to look like Frank's work, wasn't it? All right, you didn't rise to that bait, so poor Angela Sykes had to be thrown in as well. And here you are, all interested in Barbara's death again. So it worked."

"Who would want to do a thing like that to your brother? You're saying that someone killed two women with the aim of implicating your brother?"

She had begun to shake her head impatiently before he finished. She dragged on her new cigarette. "I told you I'm not stupid. No, the one who killed them wanted those two women dead. But he also wanted the deaths blamed on Frank. That could be simply to divert attention from himself. Or it could be something deeper. A vendetta."

"Did your brother consult you about his wife's funeral?" It seemed best to switch ground. Nancy Rooney was talking like someone with a theory and Horvath agreed with Keegan that theories are more of an obstacle than a help.

"How do you mean?"

"The little ceremony at the funeral home, the sad little scene at graveside."

"Without a priest? Yes. I told you, Lieutenant. My brother and his wife had ceased being Catholics. God knows when the last time was that they had been in a church. Very well. We each make our choice and I don't think it should be contradicted after we are dead. Barbara chose to have nothing to do with God. At least nothing to do with the Catholic Church. It would have been hypocrisy to send her off with a big liturgical splash."

"Did you convince your brother of that?"

A small smile. "We didn't even speak of it. It went without saying."

"He did have the grave blessed."

"What?" She sat forward, studying his face to see if this was a trick.

"He asked Father Dowling of Saint Hilary's parish to bless his wife's grave."

"I don't believe it."

It was no secret, at least no one had suggested to Cy Horvath that it was. Blessing a grave is a public act anyway. Nancy Rooney was genuinely angry.

"Did Father Dowling suggest that to my brother or the other way round?"

"You'll have to ask him that."

"I shall, Lieutenant. I shall. A priest should know better."

Horvath had meant that she should ask her brother. The question made Nancy Rooney less willing to go on with their conversation and Horvath did not get a very satisfactory account from her of the kind of man her brother was.

They already knew of his professional life. Neither Anvers nor Georgie at the country club had added much to the picture of a nondescript successful young lawyer who apparently had dissatisfied or bored his wife to the extent that she had begun to run around. He was so self-absorbed he apparently had not even noticed. But there were daubs of color in the portrait, too. The man's strange insistence that Father Dowling bless his wife's grave, for one. His visit, however uncharacteristic, to the prep school he had attended in Wisconsin. And there had been something gallant in his fighting a suicide verdict on his wife's death. But Horvath had known all this before he talked with Nancy Rooney.

She came out to the car with him, hands plunged into the pockets of her corduroy coat, the merest glance at the boys still cavorting on the lawn. Her sister-in-law's blessed grave still rankled her, it was difficult to understand why. "What is Father Dowling like?" she asked. "Is he one of these new priests?"

"He's a priest," Horvath said. "The kind of priest we've always had."

"He sounds like some sort of radical to me," Nancy Rooney said. "Going around blessing apostate graves."

When Cy Horvath drove away there was something like a smile on his face as he looked forward to telling Phil Keegan that Nancy Rooney suspected the pastor of St. Hilary's of being a radical.

17

TUTTLE still could not believe it and he sat in his office, feet on his desk, Irish hat pulled low over his eyes, looking a gift horse in the mouth, so to speak.

When Delphine had told him Mr. Francis X. Rooney was on the line, Tuttle figured there were two possible explanations. Either Delphine was kidding him (unlikely — she was a painfully literal-minded woman) or someone else was. It never entered his mind that it really was Francis X. Rooney on the line. But it was. The skepticism with which Tuttle picked up his phone faded fast as his ear filled with those unmistakably sophisticated tones. He had heard Rooney in court on several occasions. The cases he argued were never before a jury and he addressed the judge with something like complicity. Surely this was a matter gentlemen could easily settle among themselves. You would have thought that taking the thing before a judge was already a breach of some demanding and un-written code of honor.

"I know your work, of course, Mr. Tuttle. You have been recommended to me as a reliable man and I would like to get together. Why don't we make it informal? Could you be at the bar at the country club at three-thirty this afternoon? Just tell them at the door you're my guest."

"Could you tell me who recommended me," Tuttle said. He had to say something. He was as used to being recommended as he was to getting clients like Francis X. Rooney.

"Captain Philip Keegan."

Keegan! What the hell was going on? The call came just before Delphine went out to lunch. Tuttle told her to bring him back a salami and cheese, he had work to do. Delphine looked at him. Never try to fool a secretary. She knew how much work he had. The aluminum-siding salesman had been released and had refused to pay Tuttle for his consoling visit to the jail.

"I never asked you to come," the man said with justification. His mistake, Tuttle admitted it. Cash on the barrelhead was the only rule. He should have seen money from that Nashville account before he said an encouraging word to that bum. Now Tuttle wanted to spend the noon hour pondering the significance of the call from Francis X. Rooney.

But when he headed for the country club at three he hadn't a clue what the call was about. Sure, Rooney's wife had been killed, but that was a matter for the police. Was Rooney himself suspected? That was nonsense for starters, but even if it weren't, Tuttle was not the man he would turn to in such a plight. Three or four Mexicans were directing blowers around the green stretch from the county road to where the country club drive curved around the tennis courts. Blown into piles, the leaves were sucked into a mulcher. Tuttle was always fascinated by machinery he didn't understand and he would have liked to park and watch the ground crew for a while. But business called.

Having parked, Tuttle went up the front steps of the club

feeling like an interloper. Once he had dreamed of becoming a member here. Later he told himself it was no bargain at all, membership fee, prices too high, and let's face it, not the same quality of membership as when Tuttle was a boy. But the fact was he could not have afforded it. Besides, he had never been asked. So he came inside the clubhouse with something of the feeling with which Tom Canty had entered the palace.

There was no receptionist. No one there to stop him, or to greet him, for that matter. As far as Tuttle could see, he had the run of the place. He walked with a little more confidence now, heading toward a murmur of voices. In the bar, Francis X. Rooney stood, a drink in his hand, apparently in conversation with the bartender and a short fat man.

"Ah, Mr. Tuttle. Just on time." Introductions all around, Anvers the manager, Vince the bartender. It was only when he was seated at a table near a window that it occurred to Tuttle that he had been introduced to the manager and bartender as to fellow employees. Rooney lifted his bourbon and water.

"Cheers. Well, you must be wondering why I called you." Tuttle nodded and dipped into his drink. Let the client speak. The client spoke. Like the introduction to manager and bartender, what he said was not unequivocally flattering. Rooney understood that Tuttle had an unusual knowledge of Fox River, special contacts. "The criminal lawyer knows what the rest of us do not," was the way Rooney summed it up, and his tone made it unclear whether he meant "criminal" to modify Tuttle or his clientele. There were aspects to his wife's death ("You know about my wife?" Tuttle nodded.) that suggested a man with Tuttle's peculiar expertise could accomplish more than the police.

"Are you sure you don't want a private investigator?"

"I leave that entirely in your discretion, Mr. Tuttle. Naturally I would prefer that as small a circle as possible be privy to your inquiries. But make use of such auxiliaries as you see fit." The prospect of an open-ended expense account as well as a handsome fee had a marvelous effect on Tuttle. He crossed his legs, he frowned out over the practice greens, he nodded sagely as he listened. Portrait of an unsuccessful lawyer contemplating a no-lose proposition. And he had the good sense to hide his eagerness from Rooney.

"What do you expect me to find out that the police haven't or won't?"

Rooney smiled. "If I knew that I wouldn't need you, would I?" The fact, if it was a fact, that Keegan had sent Rooney to him suggested that the man had been making a pest of himself.

"I gather you're not happy with the police investigation thus far?"

"The police," Rooney began, and in his mouth the word was one of contempt. "The police were about to rule my wife's death a suicide when the appearance of that wandering salesman stayed their hand. Now they are actually suggesting there is some tie between my wife's death and that of Angela Sykes. My wife was murdered in her bath. It looks as if poor Angela drove into the river while drunk. Maybe it is the presence of water in the two instances that suggests a connection to the police. In effect, I am hiring you to protect my interests, by which I mean chiefly my late wife's good name."

Loyalty to family was one emotion Tuttle sincerely understood. His dad's name was on Tuttle's door and stationery for as long as Tuttle practiced. It was why he and Peanuts got along so well. Tuttle understood the Pianone family too. It was odd to bunch Francis X. Rooney with such a group.

Peanuts Pianone was one of the main reasons Tuttle felt sure he would earn the money he would get from Rooney. Peanuts turned out to be doubly useful. He was Tuttle's pipeline into the police department, keeping the lawyer apprised of the current state of the official investigation. But Peanuts had always been that. The bonus was that the Pianones had a financial interest in the Gutter Ball and Tuttle had certain, swift, and no-bullshit knowledge of the way Barbara Rooney and Angela Sykes had hung around the place.

"How'd you like to do a little undercover work?" Tuttle asked Delphine.

His secretary gave him the fish eye. That wasn't fair. Tuttle had always kept things on a business basis with Delphine. "I dictate, you type," he had said, thumping his chest the day he hired her. "I type, you pay," she had replied. He liked her right away. And she had stayed with him through thick and thin, mainly thin. Now he told her they were definitely coming into thick. "I'd like to get you onto the expense account in a special capacity. Ovid Investigations. That's you. I'll draw up the papers."

"Ovid?"

"His family name was Nosey. A Roman poet. That way, you can bill me for the time you spend at the Gutter Ball."

"The Gutter Ball! I'm not going near that place for love or money."

"I'm only offering money. And watch out what you say. Peanuts' family has an interest in the place."

Peanuts was eating a Hershey bar, his eyes darting back and forth from the lawyer to the secretary. Peanuts didn't understand much but he would be able to give an extremely accurate account of what had been said in his presence.

"I won't do it."

Tuttle didn't want to argue. The main thing was to set up the detective agency and have an added way to dun Rooney for the investigation.

"We'll see," he said to Delphine. Alone with Peanuts, he got caught up on the Rooney and Sykes deaths. It looked as if the police were nowhere near an explanation of one, let alone both, deaths. Tuttle had heard of the man known as Willie at the Gutter Ball when he was arrested.

"Why can't they nail him with it?"

"The footprints," Peanuts said.

"Footprints! I'm defending Rooney, I establish he took a stroll along the river last week and where are they?" Peanuts didn't know. Tuttle hadn't expected that he would. The problem was that he wasn't defending Rooney. But Rooney did not want his wife's death linked with the Sykes woman. Tuttle's course seemed clear: his aim would be to pin the Sykes death on Willie. Peanuts shook his head.

"What's wrong?"

"My uncle won't like that."

It seemed the Pianones were very unhappy that the Gutter Ball was figuring in the news the way it was. They didn't mind that the place had a reputation as a kind of swinging bar. The more people thought they could meet another lonely person in the gloom of the Gutter Ball, the better. But the suggestion that your life was in danger if you went there was something else. The Pianones on the city council were agitating now for Willie's release.

Thus it was that Tuttle sat in his office, feet on his desk, Irish hat pulled low over his eyes. He had a client who could pay and who was willing to pay. And Peanuts was telling him that the obvious way to collect was closed to him. Tuttle did not want to displease the Pianones. He might end up in the river himself. A dark thought crossed his mind. Were the Pianones behind the drowning of Angela Sykes?

He tipped back his hat, a worried look on his face. Was he using Peanuts or was Peanuts assigned to keep an eye on him? A fee for failure from Rooney would be more than Tuttle usually earned, but he did not want a potential bonanza to get away. Here was a dilemma and Tuttle did not like it. He swung his feet off his desk.

"Delphine!" he called. The walls were so thin he did not need an intercom to summon his secretary. "Delphine, get your pad in here."

18

WAS IT only his imagination that she had become his accomplice? It was difficult to say. Wanda did seem shocked when he said he intended to stop by the funeral parlor and pay his respects.

"I've never been to a funeral." She had been too young to attend her parents'. She didn't seem to know whether to be ashamed or proud of this. Martin Olson assured her that while not pleasant, it was not always a difficult occasion. He said this without reckoning on the emotions of Gerald Sykes. The bereaved ex-husband was weeping openly when Martin Olson arrived with Wanda. She had put her arm through his and he had left it there, wondering if she were exacting that small payment for her knowledge of what he had done. Wanda's arm stiffened in his at the sight of the weeping Sykes. There were not half a dozen others in the room. Martin Olson recognized several people from the country club, but employees, not members. There was Anvers, the manager, and Georgie from the pro shop. Good God, the pro was here too. Olson freed himself from Wanda and went with outstretched hand to Fairwell.

"Terrible thing," the pro muttered, his eyes darting toward Sykes.

"I thought you were in Florida."

"I was," Fairwell said. "I was."

Sykes threw his arms around Olson as if they had been close friends. He continued to cry, theatrically, wetly, contagiously. Olson saw Wanda's lower lip tremble. Georgie's eyes were damp and Anvers looked acutely uncomfortable. Olson's eye was drawn inexorably toward the open casket. He moved toward it and now it was Gerald Sykes who clung to his arm.

Angela looked waxen and unreal, her head lying on a silken pillow, her hair in a formal and uncharacteristic style. He looked at the hands folded sedately beneath her breast. He looked at his own hands and saw there the scratch Angela had made while he was injecting her with Novocain. Drunk as she was, Angela had not gone easily and Martin Olson admired her for that. When she turned and saw him in the back seat of her car she had let out a scream. Maybe the scare had sobered her up and after he had sunk the needle behind her ear he had had to hold her for ten or fifteen minutes before the Novocain took hold. That had been the worst part, crouching beside her in the car, holding his breath when there was the sound of a car on the river road. He had no way of knowing if the car was visible where it had come to a stop. He had turned off the lights as soon as he could. How quiet it was. At first she had whimpered against the hand he pressed to her mouth, but then she was silent. He could hear the leaves stirring in the trees around the car. It was a wonder the car hadn't struck a tree after it jumped the curb. They had traveled twenty yards before Olson managed to switch off the ignition. Ahead of the car there seemed to be a clear track to the river, by way of a sheer drop, that is. A creeping sensation went over him at the thought they might have gone right on over the cliff.

† 122 †

And then he knew how he would kill her. As with Barbara Rooney, he had left room for improvisation. Before starting the car, he tramped around a bit in Frank Rooney's shoes. He pushed Angela into the passenger seat. God, she was heavy. She had not been a petite person, but she seemed to weigh a ton. He turned the key, starting the motor, and then, timing it carefully, put the gear in Drive and stepped back. He stood there watching the car gather momentum as it went toward the river. At the edge of the cliff it seemed to hesitate, dipping forward, hesitating, rocked a bit, and then just slipped out of sight. There was a distant not very loud splashing sound and that was all.

And now here was Angela, all done up by the mortician, on display for mourning. Clinging to his arm, Sykes wailed like a banshee.

"How long were you married to her?" Olson asked. It seemed a way of reminding Sykes that, after all, Angela had divorced him. What was he to Hecuba or Hecuba to him? Martin Olson patted Sykes's shoulder and Sykes threw his arms about him.

"I am responsible," Sykes was blubbering. "It's all my fault."

Olson felt uneasy. There was a note of mockery in Sykes's self-accusation. Nor did he like the startled expression on Wanda's face. Olson maneuvered Sykes toward a chair and got him seated. He turned away to face Georgie.

"He keeps saying that, Doc. He doesn't mean it. He doesn't know what he's saying."

Olson nodded, avoiding Georgie's eye. It was one thing to have Wanda trading knowing looks with him, but Georgie was a long-standing pain in the neck. It was that poem Georgie had been writing for Barbara that explained it. Rather than hate Olson for humiliating him, Georgie seemed to think they had entered into a pact together. Funny kid, except that he wasn't a kid. Imagine him showing up for Angela's wake. He had been at Barbara's funeral too.

"I went over to see Sykes when Fairwell called." Georgie shook his head. "I haven't been able to get away from him since."

"It's a great loss," Martin Olson said, and Georgie, reminded of the somberness of the occasion, nodded. Martin Olson went to where Wanda had slumped into a chair at the rear of the viewing room.

"Do you want to see the deceased?" She looked up at him with terrified eyes and shook her head.

"I want to go," she said, saying each word very distinctly.

He didn't blame her, but he wanted to stay a few minutes longer. He sat in a chair next to Wanda and realized that his feeling was much like that he had after performing a particularly difficult piece of oral surgery and doing it well. The body in the casket was his handiwork. Thought of in that way, it did not seem ghoulish to take pride in what he had done. First Barbara, now Angela. He had killed them both deliberately, but in each case he had left open the possibility that he would not go through with it. He liked the mixture of careful preparation and improvisation; it was as though he were two people, the man he had become and someone he might have been, someone more like his father. It was that second, undeveloped side of himself that had thought of the note and the confusion about the typewriters, as if suspicion must fall on Rooney. The Martin Olson whose drive had taken him to wealth knew that was an unlikely outcome. But the very mixture of care and caprice had indeed confused the police.

Much the same mixture of outlooks had been involved in the killing of Angela. He had left far more room for improvising in her case. All he had decided was that he would first render her unconscious with Novocain, as he had Barbara. Angela had put up a struggle, but then he had come upon Barbara in bed, deep in drunken slumber. He had wakened her with the injection, an odd reversal of some fairy story. It had been a cold and uncomfortable wait in the back seat of Angela's car outside the Gutter Ball. He could not nap; any sound made him instantly alert. He was prepared for her to emerge with a man, thus complicating his task, but she had come out alone.

His newly discovered paternal side had welcomed the risk involved in rendering his victims inert with an injection of Novocain into the brain. Not that Novocain itself left a trace; it was the mark of the needle. But the risk was diminished because the puncture was lost among the hair at the nape of the neck. As a dentist, he liked the thought that the deaths of the two women had been painless. They had been in their way mercy killings.

A middle-sized man with a compassionate look and a case of five-o'clock shadow came into the viewing room, glanced toward the weeping Sykes and then went rapidly to him. Here was a man who would bring some semblance of dignity and decorum to the proceedings. It emerged that he was the rabbi. Sykes's sobbing had subsided when Olson and Wanda left.

Dark had fallen, the days grew shorter. The quiet pride he had felt inside seemed to dissipate when Martin Olson came outside.

"Where shall we eat?"

"I made reservations at Tim's," Wanda said. Her arm was in his again, possessively. Martin Olson had mentioned dinner as a surprise, but Wanda had surprised him. Reservations? How confident she was. She walked very close beside him, her hip bumping against him. He was both repelled and intrigued by this signal of availability. Wanda? It didn't seem as implausible as he would have thought. But then he seemed not to have much choice.

19

SOMETIMES when Josephine looked at her daughter Debbie, aged thirteen, she felt that they were sisters rather than what they were, daughter and deserted mother. It wasn't that Josephine felt sorry for herself, she honestly didn't. She couldn't deny that she had once been married to a man named Fred and that Debbie was his daughter, but her memories of those days were faded. What she felt was young, as if the years just hadn't taken any kind of toll on her. Thirty-four. Sometimes, in front of the mirror, she would say that to herself, aloud, if she was alone in the house. "You are thirty-four." But it was no more credible than if she told herself she was the Queen of Rumania.

She had stayed young by not feeling sorry for herself, by not expecting anyone to take care of her. She had waited on tables and eventually became a bartender when she saw what a deal they had. At least they stayed more or less in the same place while waitresses were running from kitchen to dining room and back, over and over. It was kind of a laugh too, since she had had to produce I.D. until she was thirty before anyone would serve her. The first time behind a bar she really got the looks.

In a place like the Gutter Ball she could really have been thirteen and no one would have noticed. What a place. Maybe nobody really grows up. But it was something to see women fifty and more sit there and giggle like schoolgirls, picking up guys, no pretense of doing anything else. And they wanted some guy they could take home to bed. The clientele of the Gutter Ball would have been surprised to know that Josephine was shocked by their antics. For her, sex was sacred. It was also a memory that had faded along with Fred. No one at the bar of the Gutter Ball would have believed her if she told them there had been no one since Fred had left her and that was eleven years ago, going on twelve. She couldn't imagine letting some semistranger sleep with her and it wasn't just because she wouldn't want Debbie to know. Debbie might approve.

Josephine was worried about Debbie, who had matured so fast. All Josephine asked was that she finish high school. It was her own big regret that she had not stayed to get her diploma. Marrying Fred had seemed a far more important thing to do at the time. It was concern over Debbie and feeling a bit ashamed about being a bartender, particularly at a place like the Gutter Ball, that had made Josephine religious.

She had been raised religious, she had always known there is a God and she was going to have to square accounts with Him one day, but she had never been saved. One Sunday morning she turned on the television and there was the Reverend Seely talking as if he could see her and was speaking directly into her heart. She put down her coffee cup and sat there staring at the screen and then she was nodding her head in agreement with Reverend Seely. He certainly had the condition of her soul down to a tee. His open Bible lay on the palm of one hand and he pointed the index finger of the other straight at her. And she had to answer No to his question. She had not made her decision for Jesus. She had not decided to put her life in the hands of the Lord.

Well, the upshot was that she went down to Salvation Tabernacle to hear Reverend Seely in person. Her first thought was that he had been more impressive on television. Even there in the Tabernacle he addressed the cameras more than he did the people seated before him. In another way he was better in person. In the Tabernacle when she began to nod in answer to his questions, when she began to say Amen, she was doing what dozens of others all around her were doing. There was a rhythm to it, Reverend Seely hollering out his questions and the rest of them saying Amen and Alleluia, swaying in their seats and stamping on the floor and when he asked those who wanted to be saved to come down the aisle and make their declaration for Jesus, Josephine did not hesitate a minute.

She had thought she would just look in and, if things looked right, come back a few times and then, who knew, maybe she would step forward, and here she was on her first visit going down the aisle, belting out a hymn, and about as happy as she had ever been in her life. That day she got religion and she got it good.

It made her even more anxious about Debbie and less comfortable behind the bar at the Gutter Ball. The people she was serving were the very children of perdition Reverend Seely preached about, and Josephine was filled with fear, wondering how she dared hope to escape the destruction that was to come. It was hard to tell from Reverend Seely's sermons how close it was, but it was pretty clear that anybody who wasn't ready for the end of the world was making a very big mistake. Josephine felt alternately excited and frightened at the thought of fire and brimstone raining down on the earth. The thing to do was to think of the next thing, Jesus coming in glory to separate the sheep from the goats.

There were nights when she wanted to do a little preaching herself, from behind the bar of the Gutter Ball. She wanted to at least whisper about the wrath that was to come. And then the wrath did come. First there was Barbara. Josephine hadn't known her full name until she read about it in the paper, the clipping that Angie brought in. It seemed a sign. Josephine wasn't blind; she knew Barbara had been married, and she knew Barbara came to the Gutter Ball seeking partners in adultery. And she was cruelly slain. It was like a judgment of the Lord. When Angie talked about it, sad and all, Josephine waited for her to see what it meant, to say it, but she didn't. Angie seemed to think Barbara's death was just an accident, not a punishment. Josephine hadn't known what instrument God had used until Angie too was struck down.

It had been a pretty disgraceful night, the little man called Willie making a fool of himself, he and Angie drinking, drinking, and then Willie had tripped and crashed the piano against Bobby. Then Angie and Willie left together. That's what everyone thought. That's what everyone told Agnes Lamb, the cop who had done the interviewing. But Josephine knew otherwise.

She had seen Angie waiting for Willie to come out of the john. And she had seen her finally give up on him. More importantly, when she was outside getting a breath of air during her break, she had seen the man in the back seat of Angie's car. She recognized him as the man who had been seated back against the wall. Josephine had gotten used to the dimness of the bar and she liked to know who was seated out there in the dark. Maybe she half feared that some backslider from the Tabernacle would come in some night and see her behind the bar.

She didn't know who the man was. She didn't know what he was doing in the back seat of Angie's car. He might simply have been a drunken patron who crawled in there for the stupid reason drunks have for doing the stupid things they do. But the next day Josephine understood.

That man had been the instrument of the divine wrath. She knew then she had seen him somewhere before and she wracked her brain trying to remember. It could have been at the Tabernacle but somehow she didn't think so. He had been at the Gutter Ball before, she was sure of that, but that must have been because of Barbara. If she hadn't realized that the man was doing the Lord's work she would have told Officer Lamb about him. As it was, he was beyond the reach of the law. Think of all the slaying and killing in the Bible, done at the behest of the Lord. It wouldn't make much sense to bring the Lord's right hand before a judge. Even when evil men fulfilled God's plan, Josephine did not see what the point of arresting them would be. Take Herod's soldiers and the slaughter of the innocents. Were those soldiers personally guilty of anything?

It was a little spooky realizing that Bible kinds of thing were happening there in the Gutter Ball. Not that anyone could claim they hadn't had fair warning. It was all there in the Bible and all a person had to do was have ears to hear. So Josephine had not told Agnes Lamb everything she might have, and she was prepared to do the same when Lieutenant Horvath came to her apartment that afternoon.

"Did I get you up or anything?" he asked.

"It's nearly two o'clock in the afternoon."

"How late do you tend bar at the Gutter Ball?"

"Until closing time."

"Three A.M. I guess you wouldn't still be in bed. I'm here to talk about your two customers who've been killed lately." He seemed to think she would have something to say about that way of putting it, but Josephine held her peace. She wondered if Lieutenant Horvath was saved. Probably not. Most cops are Catholics and she had heard all about them from Reverend Seely.

Horvath said, "Would you tell me everything you can remember about Barbara Rooney."

"Well, she drank rob roys."

"What are they?"

"Scotch and sweet vermouth, a maraschino cherry. It's a Manhattan with Scotch instead of bourbon."

Horvath made a face. "I've never understood how poeple can drink Scotch. It smells like iodine."

"I suppose it's an acquired taste."

"I suppose you could acquire a taste for iodine too. Did she drink a lot?"

"Well, I only saw her at the bar. She drank all the while she was there."

"But not everybody drinks at the same rate, do they?"

"No."

"Where would you put Barbara Rooney on a scale. High or low?"

"High."

"Angela Sykes the same?"

"Higher."

"I don't know how you can do it."

"What do you mean?"

"Do you drink yourself?"

"No." Meaning, no more. That was part of being saved.

"So there you are, sober yourself, making drinks for people like Barbara and Angela."

"It's my job."

"It's a job. But why yours? You don't really approve of women like that, do you?"

"No!" The answer jumped out the way answers did when Reverend Seely put his questions.

"Neither do I," Lieutenant Horvath said. His wide expressionless face was reassuring. Josephine did not feel she had made a dangerous admission since his expression had not changed. "Barbara Rooney had a husband and two kids. Angela Sykes was divorced, but even so." Horvath looked away. "Myself, I don't believe in divorce."

"What God has joined together."

"Yes."

The only trouble with that was it meant Fred was still her

husband. The Bible said a man could put away his wife on account of adultery but it wasn't clear if a wife could do the same. That would have made it all right about Fred because the chance of his not living with another woman was zero. Josephine liked Lieutenant Horvath. They saw things the same way.

"Aren't you a Catholic?" she asked him.

"Catholics aren't the only people who don't believe in divorce."

Josephine nearly laughed. She was about to tell Horvath about Catholics when he said, "But I am a Catholic." Ye gods, what if she had repeated what Reverend Seely told her!

"I'm drinking tea," she said, "but I could make you a cup of instant if you want coffee."

"I would like a cup." He came with her into the kitchen. He seemed even bigger there. They waited for the water to boil and she told him about Debbie. He was very easy to talk to, maybe because she wanted to get some response from him. But even though his expression never really changed, she had the feeling that he was interested in what she was saying, really interested, not just a guy on the make who would act as if he couldn't hear enough about your day and everything when all along all he wanted...

"Do you have kids, Lieutenant?" He shook his head and that was all, but he might have confided a great tragedy to her. Josephine felt truly sorry for him. Having Debbie was one of the nicest things that had ever happened to her. A woman had to know she could have children and it was the same for a man. Josephine was sure that being childless was the biggest cross Lieutenant Horvath had to bear.

"Angela Sykes had no kids," Horvath said. "So she wasn't hurting them. But her ex-husband may never recover from this."

"Lot had to just leave his wife and continue on his way. The fault was not his."

Horvath nodded. "That's true. If I'm a Catholic, what are you? You brought it up."

"I'm a Christian."

"What kind?"

She smiled. Reverend Seely made fun of these contests among the churches. He himself preached the simple Christian message.

"I attend services at Salvation Tabernacle."

"Reverend Heely?"

"Seely. How did you know that?"

"I've seen him on television."

"What do you think?"

Horvath shrugged. "He's better than a lot of them. I'm surprised he lets you tend bar."

"He doesn't know." She had to protect Reverend Seely. She didn't want Lieutenant Horvath to think Reverend Seely was a respecter of persons or one who trimmed the gospel for any reason whatever. But he couldn't be too strict for Josephine. The water came to a boil, she made his cup of coffee and another cup of tea for herself and they went back into the front room. He stopped before the picture of Jesus she had hanging on the wall, one she really liked. The eyes followed you wherever you went. Josephine found it a great comfort.

"That picture told me you were not a typical bartender," Lieutenant Horvath said. "You were going to tell me all about Barbara Rooney."

He was a little tricky, no doubt about that, but then it was his job and she didn't really resent it. But she had made no promise to tell him all about Barbara Rooney and he knew it. What she did tell him he would have known already.

"Those two were asking for it," Lieutenant Horvath said after a time, shaking his head. "How could they possibly have known enough about the men they went off with?"

"It's an odd atmosphere, that bar. Within minutes they're acting as if they'd known each other forever."

"You must get some creepy types though. Sexually creepy."

"That's not really true. I was a bit surprised to learn that Barbara and Angie belonged to the country club, but only a bit. The men all wear suits and ties, salesmen mainly. In one sense, they're pretty high-class people."

"Well, one of them is a murderer."

Josephine sipped her tea and said nothing. Would Abraham have been a murderer if he had killed Isaac? Still and all, she decided, if the police caught the man, then that was what God wanted. But since she didn't know that was what He wanted she could not be of any real help to Lieutenant Horvath.

20

MARIE MURKIN was not often intimidated but when Nancy Rooney bore down on the St. Hilary rectory and demanded to see the pastor, she was given no crash course in the daily demands on the time of Father Dowling. She was not even put in a front parlor to wait while Marie came to tell the pastor he had a caller and make a guess or two as to the reason for the visit. Roger Dowling looked up from his breviary to see two women in the doorway of his study, Marie and a woman of perhaps fifty of patrician mien.

"Father Dowling, I am Nancy Rooney."

And into the room she sailed, a gloved hand extended to the priest. He rose and took it.

"How do you do? You are the second Rooney I've had come visit me lately." He narrowed his eyes and smiled. "The other I would guess is your brother."

"That's right. And that brings us directly to the point."

Nancy Rooney cast a dismissing glance at Marie Murkin, who still stood in the doorway looking like a sentry through whose post the enemy had flooded. Roger Dowling nodded reassuringly and Marie withdrew to the kitchen. Nancy Rooney sat down in the chair Father Dowling indicated and looked sternly at the pastor. "I am told that you blessed my sister-in-law's grave. Or should it be sister's-in-law?"

"The first. Yes, I blessed Barbara Rooney's grave."

"May I ask why?"

"Are you asking the purpose of a blessing or the reason for this one?"

"Barbara believed as much in blessings as she did in reincarnation."

"I didn't know her."

"All the more reason why blessing her grave was inappropriate."

"Her husband requested it. He didn't want a big fuss made of it. I'm surprised he even told you about it."

"That he should make the request is what mystifies me. He and Barbara had long since stopped going to Mass or receiving the sacraments. What restrictions on blessings are there?"

"Who knows what went through your sister-in-law's mind during the last moments of her life?"

Nancy Rooney made an impatient noise. "A deathbed conversion? Not Barbara, Father. I assure you. Since her death we have been learning some rather sad things about her life."

"You must have grown up in this parish, didn't you?"

"Yes. We all did. Frank and I. Barbara too. Frank got the old family house. So you would have known the two of them if they had remained Catholics."

"Your brother came to me as a parishioner, more or less."

The alteration in manner at the mention of childhood was soon gone. Roger Dowling found Nancy Rooney a difficult woman to understand. He wasn't sure he could like anyone who intimidated Marie Murkin.

"I walked down past your brother's house the other day. It's such a shame, those nice old houses and neighborhoods, isolated by the freeways."

"It is even sadder when you think how little such a house would bring, even on today's market. If for no other reason, I'm glad Frank chose to live there."

"Will he sell it now?"

"Why should he?"

Roger Dowling shrugged. "I was thinking of the children. He is very fortunate to have you for a sister. I understand you've been looking after the children."

"They are my nephews, Father. It is scarcely a chore." She took out a cigarette and lit it. It might have been a way to change the subject. "What exactly did my brother say when he came wanting a blessing for Barbara's grave?"

"What did he say he said?"

She looked at him. "Frank is not my source of information on this matter."

"Really?"

"A policeman told me."

Well, well. That meant Phil Keegan, not that it had been told him as a secret. Phil or Horvath must have seen what a rise it would get from Nancy Rooney to be told about the blessing. But why should it bother her?

"May I ask if you yourself are still a Catholic?"

For answer she gave him a list of her credentials: Daughters of Isabella, Christ Child Society, The Legion of Mary, the parish Benevolent Society. Roger Dowling, smiling helplessly, held up a hand to stop the inventory.

"I tell you because you ask. The Rooneys have always been staunch Catholics. It has not been easy to remain a Catholic, at least an enthusiastic one, during these past several years. So much nonsense. I don't suggest that that is why my brother and his wife stopped going to church but I know many people who simply could not bear the liturgical shenanigans anymore. You must wonder why I seem concerned over your blessing Barbara's grave. That is your answer. I am so weary of having important things treated as if they do not matter. But surely either someone believes in God or he does not. If not, that decision should be respected, after death as well as before. It seems only simple honesty to me."

"I understand that. But when a man asks me to bless his wife's grave I assume he sees some point in the request."

"I am afraid it was meant to placate me. Frank took my silence about the funeral arrangements he made to be criticism. I was saddened but I did not disapprove. My concern is rather for the religious education of my nephews."

"Ah."

"Frank quite agrees they should be raised Catholic." She sighed. "I will never understand how he can be so casual about such matters. I would respect him more if he fought me."

"Miss Rooney, how did your sister-in-law die?"

"How? She committed suicide."

"I think that theory has been discarded."

"By the police?" Nancy Rooney smiled. "They resist the obvious because they cannot find the instrument with which she cut her wrists. Now they must produce a stranger with a curious penchant for writing typed notes. I prefer to be mystified by the absence of the razor blade. Since I believe she did commit suicide, you will see I have yet another reason to disapprove of blessing her grave."

"Did you know Angela Sykes?"

"Oh yes. I was acquainted with her. And I catch your point. But the effort to link Barbara's death and that of Angela Sykes seems to me just more idle speculation."

"You mentioned things that have come out concerning the way your sister-in-law lived."

"I realize she went out on the town with Angela. As I told Lieutenant Horvath, I myself witnessed Barbara's behavior during her Mrs. Hyde nights. It was disgusting. But that is neither here nor there. Angela seems to have lost her way while driving drunk."

"Did Lieutenant Horvath say anything to you of a footprint near where Angela Sykes went into the river?"

But Nancy Rooney was not interested in speculating about the death of Angela Sykes. There was much to admire in the woman, Father Dowling thought, but much that was unsympathetic. Nancy Rooney acted as though she would be disappointed to hear that her sister-in-law had indeed repented in the last moments of her life. Satisfied apparently that she had chided Roger Dowling for what she regarded as his indiscriminate scattering of God's mercy, she put out her third cigarette and rose. Roger Dowling went with her to the door and, the day being a pleasant one, continued with her to her car. Nancy stood for a moment, her glance going from the church to what had been the parish school.

"I spent eight years there," she said. Again her expressive sigh. "This was such a great parish then." Nostalgia? Criticism? Perhaps a bit of both. Roger Dowling was not used to being numbered among the mad innovators who annoyed and scandalized the faithful. But he must not take pleasure in the fact that he displeased Nancy Rooney. He watched her drive away, then walked to the church to make a visit.

In midafternoon, the huge empty church did suggest that it had seen its better days. People had moved from the area with the arrival of the highways and interstates, following the national trend into the suburbs. St. Hilary parish became a triangular island whose inhabitants could hear both day and night the muted sound of traffic, eastbound, westbound. There were not many young couples with children left, so the school had been transformed into a parish center catering to the elderly and the retired. Roger Dowling could imagine the parish simply becoming obsolete. But it was always unwise to predict such things. He could also think that, in a way, the parish had known a kind of renaissance in recent years. And there were a few young couples who had moved into the area, attracted by the large and relatively inexpensive homes to be found there. There might be need for a parish school again if the trend continued.

He walked down the center aisle of the church, genuflected, and knelt in a pew. He lowered his face into his hands, intent on praying, but a distracting image formed in the darkness. One woman bleeding to death in her bathtub scarcely more than a mile from where he now knelt; another drowning in the river. And the two women had been friends. Not a full month had passed between the death of the one and the death of the other. Surely Nancy Rooney was wrong in thinking there was no connection between the two deaths. He sat back in the pew. Rather than fight these distracting thoughts, he decided to concentrate on them. One thing that had emerged from the trip he had taken to Wisconsin with Phil Keegan was that Frank Rooney could certainly have come home to Fox River before he said he had. From the point of view of opportunity, there was nothing to prevent his having killed his wife. And, if one were to be skeptical about what Frank Rooney claimed, his ignorance of his wife's extracurricular affairs came into doubt. And that gave him motive. He had not become a suspect because of his alibi—he had been out of town and arrived home at midmorning to find his dead wife. And immediately telephoned the police. Frank Rooney, as murderer? It was hard to believe that any husband could be so unaware of what his wife was doing or could dismiss the evidence of it in as untroubled a way as Frank Rooney apparently had. If he knew of it, it would certainly have enraged him.

Father Dowling was not really surprised that Nancy Rooney had not mentioned the obvious explanation of the missing razor on the assumption that Barbara Rooney had committed suicide. Frank's adamant refusal to accept a verdict of suicide had been the most powerful point in favor of his innocence. And, feeling that strongly about it, it was plausible to think he had himself disposed of the razor blade. But that is also something he would have done on the assumption that he himself was the killer. Then the absent blade, the mystifying note in the typewriter, his insistence that his wife was murdered and the request that her grave be blessed, were elements in an effort to obfuscate and confuse. And what then of the death of Angela Sykes? If one took Frank Rooney as the killer, he could certainly be taken to be Angela's slayer as well. She was the woman who had led his wife astray. Perhaps Angela had come to suspect that Frank had killed his wife and thus presented a danger to him. That seemed something to hang onto in any case. Whoever had killed Angela had done so because she represented a threat; she must have known who had killed Barbara Rooney and she could have known it without realizing she did. Had anyone interviewed her before she herself was killed?

Phil Keegan shook his head when Roger Dowling put the question to him that night when the two men were playing pinochle in the pastor's study.

"Where was she on the night Barbara Rooney was killed?"

"With Barbara Rooney. Early in the evening. They had dinner together."

"How do you know that?"

"I already told you. A dentist named Olson. He ran into them at the restaurant and they asked him to eat with them. Afterward, he parted from them."

"Is that Martin Olson?"

"Do you know him?"

"No. But he is Marie Murkin's dentist. Not her regular dentist. But she was referred to him. He is an oral surgeon, isn't he, your Olson?"

Keegan nodded. "The two women then went to the Gutter Ball together."

"How late is that place open?"

"Well, it's supposed to close at three in the morning." This information had not been had before Angela died. Horvath had managed to find out about the visit to the Gutter Ball of the two women on the last night of Barbara Rooney's life. If they had known it earlier, if they had been able to talk with Angela Sykes, they might know who had killed Barbara and Angela might still be alive. Arresting the itinerant aluminum-siding man from Tennessee had been as useless as arresting the man called Willie who had spent the last hours of Angela's life with her at the Gutter Ball. The bartender there had finally corroborated his story that he had not gone off with Angela. Angela had been seen leaving alone.

"That's the current note, Roger. The Gutter Ball. It links the two women but how it links their deaths I don't know. I'm beginning to think Rooney's mad stranger may be the way to go after all. Imagine the creeps that hang around a bar like that, Roger. Sexual maniacs in among the womanizers and grass widows and alcoholics. Why not? Jack the Ripper. He kills Barbara. He kills Angela."

"And will kill again. Have you taken any safeguards against that?"

"I've got Agnes Lamb doing some undercover work there. And Peanuts." Keegan made a face. "He was Robertson's idea. Because of the Pianone connection with the place. Agnes is okay. She's a woman and she's black, but she's okay. As for Peanuts, forget it. And now that bastard Tuttle is involved. Pardon my French."

"Is it really true that Frank Rooney is Tuttle's client?"

"Rooney knows Tuttle is shady so he thinks he will have a shady enough insight into what happened to Barbara Rooney."

"Then he accepts the fact that his wife was being unfaithful to him?"

Keegan shrugged. "Search me. But he has Tuttle looking into the Gutter Ball. Imagine Peanuts and Tuttle tripping over each other in the dark. Whatever Agnes might have accomplished down there will be screwed up by those two."

It was a melancholy thought, people roaming about into the morning hours in search of diversion. The life of pleasure seemed to demand strenuous and painful exertion: sitting in noisy smoked-filled places like the Gutter Ball, drinking too much, bored and sleepy. It sounded like punishment to Roger Dowling.

"Your deal, Roger."

"Sorry," the priest said and began to distribute the cards.

21

WANDA looked over the shoulder of Catherine the receptionist and saw that the waiting room was full. There were two add-ons this afternoon, emergencies Dr. Olson could not refuse, since they were sent to him by dentists who regularly referred their surgery to him. There was no way they could be out of the clinic before six. They would be late for their reservation time. No matter. She would change it. She picked up the phone and dialed the number of Tim's. For the first time in her relationship with Martin Olson Wanda was in charge.

He has delivered himself into my hands. This somewhat dramatic statement of the way things were had occurred to her the night before, lying in her bed, waiting for Martin to come to her. He spent an awful long time in the bathroom, nervous as a bride. It was difficult to believe that he had murdered two women. When he did come to her, having turned off all the lights, banging against things in the dark, he seemed to tremble as she received him in her arms. She felt no danger at all. The women he had killed had spurned him, made fun of him. Wanda had been waiting for years for him to see her as a woman and not simply as his clinic manager. With her, Martin would learn how to love. They had not talked of the deaths of Barbara Rooney and Angela Sykes. That was not necessary. She knew, he knew she knew. He has delivered himself into my hands.

Holding the trembling dentist, she wondered if he feared being found out. That must not happen. Wanda did not intend to lose Martin now that she had him.

At the restaurant she said, "You had dinner here with Barbara and Angela, the night Barbara died."

It was time to let him know how profoundly they were linked. Martin looked both angry and frightened. For a moment she thought he would seek to deny it. But of course Wanda was not the only one who knew about his dinner with the two condemned women. "That was a terrible coincidence. I would rather not talk about it." That was a course they might have taken. It was the course they had been on, to this point. A wordless pact to dissemble and pretend. If what she knew was never expressed, it was thereby less real. That course no longer appealed. What he had done had given Wanda her leverage and she would have been a fool not to use it. "Martin, I know." It was a musical phrase: his name pronounced distinctly, in a normal tone of voice, the pronoun thin, but held for three, four beats, and then the dying fall of the verb. The words were more intimate than the clumsy union of the night before. His eyes searched hers, tried to look away and could not, for she held them, forcing him to understand. Slowly he nodded his head.

"You can talk about it with me, Martin. You have to talk about it with someone."

He looked around the dining room, at the other tables, at the waiters, at the trio providing dinner music for the diners, as if Wanda were inviting him to make public confession of what he had done. She put out her hand, enclosing one of his. "I am your accomplice, Martin. I am your partner."

All he could do was nod, but Wanda thought she detected the beginning of relief in his manner. How badly he must want to confide in someone what he had done.

"I am your partner," she repeated. He did not speak to her of it that night, though later in her arms he wept uncontrollably. She found that she was not really surprised at his inadequacy. In lieu of a love life Wanda had read books, and she had a bookish knowledge of the intimacies that take place, or fail to take place, between men and women. That did not matter, not now. Things would get better.

Two days later, on a Sunday, they had dinner at the country club. When they left, he took her home with him. It was there, sitting before the fireplace with its intimate fire, drinking brandy, that he spoke of it.

"You should know that Mrs. Rooney suffered less pain that morning than she did when I operated on her in the clinic. I first rendered her inert with Novocain."

"You gave her an injection?"

He nodded. Wanda frowned at the flickering flames. Had that been noticed when the coroner examined the body? The question continued to pick at her mind so that she paid less attention than she might have to Martin's account of the death of Barbara Rooney. He too seemed able to regard it in an antiseptic way. He had put the limp and naked Mrs. Rooney into her bath. The note? Martin expected her applause of the note he had left in the typewriter; Wanda thought it more foolish than shrewd. "Fingerprints?" He shook his head and the brandy in his glass moved intricately, leaving translucent layers of itself on the convex bell of his glass. "I wore surgical gloves. I put them on in the car. I was very careful."

He had not really expected suspicion to remain with Frank

Rooney. Wanda said, "Everything would have been much simpler if they had ruled her death a suicide."

Martin was silent. He seemed displeased by the remark. A full minute went by before he spoke.

"It would have been better for Angela, yes." Once he was used to the fact that he could speak freely with her, a note of pride came into his voice as he spoke of the deaths of the two women. He calculated that he may have deprived the women of little more than a decade of life. The way they lived, it was conceivable they would have met with an accident. "They picked up strangers, Wanda. They had no idea who those men were. That last night, after they left Tim's, they went on to a bar and picked up two men. Eventually they took them home to Angela's." While Martin followed them about? He must have waited in the night outside Angela's for Barbara to come out. Wanda did not like to think of him lurking in the shadows or waiting shivering in his car while in the house the two women carried on with their strangers.

"If you didn't know, no one would," he said softly.

"You're sure the police won't ever suspect you?"

"If they do, I can deflect their attention."

"How?"

He would not say. It might have been brandy-induced bravura.

Wanda did not care. He had confided in her at last. He was convinced that she alone knew what he had done. The syllogism that formed in her head seemed to transfer to his. If Wanda was the only one who knew what he had done, she must be made safe.

"And now we must marry," he murmured.

"Are you asking me?"

"Yes."

"I accept."

She turned her face to him and they kissed, but it was like

sealing a bargain. Of course he wanted to marry her. How better silence the one witness against him?

Unless he chose to murder her as well. If marrying would provide him with protection against her possible testimony, she would need to neutralize the attraction her definitive silence might exercise on him. Somehow she must record a conversation like the one they had just had.

22

GEORGIE had never before seen the woman Dr. Olson had had his dinner with at the country club that evening. Maggie Regan waited on them but she just shrugged at Georgie's question and tossed off the half drink Dr. Olson's companion had left on the table. When she was done she wiped her mouth in an unladylike manner.

"They're real good friends, Georgie. I can tell you that. Head to head all night."

Georgie had noticed that, almost with disapproval. He had thought of himself and Olson as the true mourners for Barbara Rooney. God knows Mr. Rooney seemed to have adjusted to his loss quickly enough. It was Georgie's theory that Mr. Rooney had killed Barbara. Of course he would get off. They weren't going to put a Rooney on trial in Fox River. Rooney had an alibi and that must be a relief to the cops. The more Georgie brooded on it, the more angry he grew. It wasn't right. Nobody should be allowed to get away with murder. Not even Mr. Rooney. And whoever killed Barbara Rooney should pay for it with his own life. Georgie had wanted to discuss this with Dr. Olson. The fact that the oral surgeon had confiscated his poem, once the cause of bitter and embarrassed anger, now was a link between them. It would enable them to discuss the Barbara Rooney case man to man. The police investigation did not seem to go beyond that single visit of Horvath to the club. Olson would agree with him that Francis X. Rooney should not be permitted to kill his wife and walk around a free man.

But Dr. Olson was a difficult man to have a casual conversation with. Georgie had called his clinic and asked to speak with the dentist but, told to state the reason for his call, he had hung up, intimidated by the woman's imperious voice. He began to think he would have to make an appointment at the clinic to see Olson. Olson did not come to the club and Georgie had not wanted to telephone him at his home. But he had done it anyway. No one had answered the phone. Now Olson's companion in the country club dining room seemed to explain it all.

The woman wasn't all that much to look at. Certainly not in the same league as Barbara Rooney or even Angela Sykes. Her face was thin, her nose prominent, and when she smiled, as she did most of the time, her teeth hung over her lower lip. Not exactly the sort of woman with whom Olson might seek to drown his memories of Barbara Rooney. Besides, it was the woman who was doing the drinking, not Olson.

"She works for him," Anvers said impatiently. "She manages the clinic. Why do you ask?"

Georgie didn't answer. To hell with Anvers. He went downstairs to the hideaway and tipped back in his chair and meditated. It looked as if he was the only one who remained loyal to the memory of Barbara Rooney and not much more than a month had passed since she died. Thirty-six days to be exact, and Georgie could be exact.

† 150 †

At home he heard more about Barbara Rooney than he wanted to. His mother got a big kick out of the fact that two women who had been members of the country club had come to violent ends. She seemed to think it was the fault of the country club. Of course all she really wanted to do was bug Georgie. She knew how proud he was of his job and those two murders gave her a weapon. "Oh pardon me," she would correct herself. "I mean one suicide and one murder."

Georgie knew better than to rise to that bait. The first time she spoke of Barbara Rooney's death as suicide, Georgie had objected. He should have known better than to hand that to her. "They could both be suicides, for that matter." Georgie lifted the sports page higher, blocking from view his mother and sister. God how he hated the time he spent at home.

Right now he could fall asleep in the hideaway, his chair was as comfortable as his bed at home. But if he did, his mother would phone and wonder what had become of him. Georgie wouldn't give her the satisfaction of reminding people at the club that Georgie still had to account to his mother for his whereabouts. If the woman with Olson worked for him, she didn't mean anything. They would have been talking business, that's what they had had their heads together about.

Georgie touched the lever of his chair and brought himself upright. Why not go to Olson's house, drop in, just assume the dentist would want to talk about Barbara Rooney? Georgie could have a beer or two first. Not so much for Dutch courage as to provide an excuse in case Olson resented his dropping in.

Georgie drank one bottle of beer and ordered another. He didn't think he would be able to down the second one. But it was the smell of beer on himself that he wanted. He spilled some on his shirt. Geez. If he weren't drinking in a bar he would have dabbed some behind his ears.

The bar featured an oversized television screen on which

the Black Hawks' game was being shown. There were a lot of hockey fans in the bar and they followed the swift fortunes of the contest with shouts and groans. Georgie had never really understood the game and he was never too sure what the cause of the excitement was. The bartender had a broken nose and a gold tooth and hadn't much cared for the interruption when Georgie asked for the second beer. Georgie would have liked some popcorn to go with the beer but it didn't seem advisable to ask. Weren't there any time-outs in hockey?

He studied himself in the mirror behind the bar. Narrow face, red hair, brown suede jacket. What had he seemed to Barbara Rooney? Olson had as much as accused him of being some kind of weirdie for liking Mrs. Rooney. But his was the anger of a jealous man. His jealousy would not have survived Mrs. Rooney. The second beer did not taste as bad as the first. The idea that he and Olson could sit down and talk about a woman they had both admired seemed less and less implausible to Georgie. Man to man. They could talk of what a great athlete she had been. That was an endless subject in itself. Georgie couldn't quite imagine himself confessing to Dr. Olson that he had loved Mrs. Rooney. Not on just two beers he couldn't.

After he finished the second beer he got off the stool. The bartender acknowledged his departure with a distracted wave. The son of a bitch didn't even look at Georgie.

Olson's house was located in one of the new suburbs on the western shore of the Fox River. After he turned into the development and followed a wide street illumined by lantern-like street lamps, he told himself that he had given Olson more than enough time to take the woman home. It was not yet eleven o'clock. The houses he passed, set far back on huge lots, glowed with lights. It was not too late to call on Olson.

He went past the driveway before he saw the number. He

pulled to the side of the road and looked over the rolling lawn to the house. In the driveway a car was parked. There were lights on in the house but the drapes were pulled. Georgie turned off his motor and cut the lights. Having come this far he did not want to give up the idea of talking with Olson. It was silly to think of the car in the driveway as an obstacle. Georgie got out of his car and started toward the house.

The night air was cool. Georgie inhaled deeply and it cleared his head. When he closed the door of his car he did it gently, just easing it shut. He felt like an intruder. He felt the way he had when Olson accused him of creeping around after Barbara Rooney. Suddenly he knew it had been a mistake to come here. The realization came too late. The dog came out of nowhere, the only fore-warning Georgie had was the guttural growl when the beast sprang.

Georgie had always been afraid of dogs. As a kid, he had worked out routes to and from school that ensured that he would not have to brave any barking dogs. But he had never before been attacked by a dog. He was startled by his own courage. The dog's teeth sank into the arm Georgie raised instinctively. He brought his closed fist down on the dog's skull, emitting as he did so a roaring shout. The dog dropped free and began a snarling circling of Georgie. "Get out of here!" he shouted. "Let me alone. Go!" Lights were turned on, doors opened and slammed, a voice began to call, "Brownie! Here, Brownie."

Georgie heard his own voice rise out of control. Fear was replacing his first unthinking reaction. His legs trembled. He was sure the dog would spring again. Its teeth were bared in a cruel and ugly way. People were coming now, he felt the center of things, a point on which the world converged. He was sweating, his breath came in gasps. He felt faint. He wanted to faint, but that goddam dog . . . A hand took control of the dog's collar and Georgie, as if released, sank into the dark.

23

HE SAT before the fire with Wanda, sipping brandy which oddly did nothing to numb his senses or cast a glow of romantic fulfillment over the scene. He had improbably proposed to Wanda and she had accepted. They would marry. There would be children perhaps. There stretched before him a prospect he had thought he wanted, what he had envied in the lives of others would now be his. In the fireplace flames glowed blue. Blue is the color of sadness. Martin Olson felt trapped. I am your partner, Wanda had said, and that had been his cue. He had not been free to ignore it. How uncomfortable it was with Wanda pressing against him. She seemed bony, muscular, not soft and pliable as he had imagined the body of a woman would be. They had slept together.

But if that seemed a bad dream, the fact that he had actually talked to Wanda about the two women he had killed was a nightmare. Good God, he had given her total power over him. The proposal had been the first thing she exacted with the power she now had. But he needed someone to talk to about what he had done. It seemed oddly worse and better in the telling. Saying it domesticated it. I killed Barbara and then I killed Angie. Something that could so easily find its way into ordinary language lost a good part of its horror. But by saying it, he had taken Wanda beyond the suspicion she had had, perhaps even her belief. Now she had his word for it.

Whatever it was he had dreamed of when he envied Frank Rooney his life with Barbara seemed parodied by this scene before the fireplace. Wanda had worked for him since he had opened the clinic. Had he ever once thought of her as he had Barbara Rooney? Or Angela Sykes, for that matter? He had cast no wondering speculative looks at Wanda. Her body beneath the starched planes of her uniform had seemed part of the furniture. No, that wasn't fair. She was as reliable as a computer, his confidante. Talking to her was like dictating into his portable cassette recorder. But if he had never looked at Wanda as he had at Mrs. Rooney, it was when Barbara became his patient that Wanda began to indicate she was more than an employee, not merely an efficient machine. That was when she started to come to work wearing street clothes rather than a uniform. Her job description was more a matter of tradition than agreement. She had grown with the clinic. To placate her when even in his own eyes he was making a fool out of himself with Barbara Rooney — he had been unable to treat her as just another patient, had done her checkups himself, had scheduled her for unnecessary weekly returns to the clinic — he had given Wanda a new title. Executive Manager of the clinic. He had raised her salary too, a very good raise, a third of what she had been making. Already he had been entering into a pact with her, and if he had not realized it, Wanda did. That was his first mistake. He had given her a power that only a saint could resist using. His excuse to himself was that he had no idea Wanda considered him anything but her employer. It came as a genuine surprise to learn that Wanda cared for him. The knowledge cheapened her. And now they would marry.

† 155 †

He drained the brandy in his glass. He did not like to drink because he feared its effect on him. He wanted to be in control. A blurred mind, a thick tongue were not Martin Olson's idea of recreation. But at the moment he felt he could welcome the numbing of his brain. Wanda moved her head against his shoulder and her hand sought his. He managed not to pull his away. Suddenly Wanda sat up. Outside, a ferocious barking began and there was the terrified sound of a man's voice. "What's that?" Her tone was more curious than frightened. Martin Olson got to his feet and walked to the front door. When he opened it his flesh crawled at the terror in the man's voice. And then he saw the man, a turning pivot as the dog circled, its guttural growl filling the suburban street. Up and down the street others were coming out to see what was going on. And then Olson realized that the man being attacked by the dog was a familiar figure. My God! It was Georgie.

Olson was not the first one to the scene. The owner took hold of the collar of the dog and Georgie slumped to the ground, apparently in a faint.

Excited chatter began among his neighbors. Was the man a prowler, a peeping tom, a kidnaper, what?

"It's Georgie," Olson said, his impatience ambiguous. Was it directed at his neighbors or at Georgie?

A woman gingerly patting the head of the now subdued dog looked at him. "You know him?"

"He works at the country club."

On the ground, Georgie began to moan. His eyes opened and he looked up at Martin Olson. Relief spread over Georgie's face and he tried to get to his feet. The dog began to snarl again, straining toward the fallen intruder. Georgie was on his feet in a single movement and took Olson's arm.

"What are you up to, Georgie?" Olson strove for a kidding tone and failed to hit it.

"I came to see you."

"At this hour?" There was the smell of stale beer on Georgie's breath. Was he drunk?

"That's my car," Georgie said, pointing to the vehicle parked on the road.

"You should have telephoned."

"I figured if you weren't free, that was okay. I was willing to take the chance. Is that your dog?"

"No!" The dislike he felt for domestic animals was conveyed to the dog's owner. It served to break up the gathering. His neighbors trailed away across the lawns and Olson was left with Georgie.

"Why did you want to see me?"

"To talk."

Georgie made it sound urgent. Olson recalled that this was the boy who had had the nerve to write a poem for Barbara Rooney. Except that Georgie wasn't a boy. Olson had the strange certainty that Georgie had come here to talk about Barbara Rooney. He glanced toward the house.

His neighbors went away like wraiths across the suburban lawns, autumn grass crackling as if frost already lay upon it. From the street, Olson thought his house looked strange, though it was much like the others in the development. Was he seeing it with Georgie's eyes now, and Wanda's? The shrubbery reached almost as high as the roof of the low ranch house. From the chimney smoke rose in a white whisper toward the night sky. His house had the look of an intruder in the peaceful suburb, but it was he who was intruded on. What was Georgie up to, coming out here at this time of the night? He had never come to the house before. Why should he? He had no business here. He was an employee of the country club.

But Martin Olson could not stir up his indignation. His own humble origins made him and Georgie fellows, no matter the successful practice, the gobs of money, the house in the suburb. And they were linked as well by Barbara Rooney. Georgie seemed as puzzled by women as Martin Olson. Georgie said he had come to talk. How ominous that seemed.

He took Georgie's elbow and led him up the driveway toward the house. Wanda waited in the open doorway. Wanda and Georgie. Suddenly Martin Olson felt bracketed by menace and he felt fear deep in his bones. His secret was not safe with Wanda. And Georgie was not as innocent as he seemed. He never had been.

24

THE CAR was discovered at six-thirty in the morning by two boys squirrel-hunting with .22s along the east bank of the Fox River south of town. The boys seemed a lot more nervous about the squirrel-hunting than about finding the bodies and Captain Keegan wondered what the hell they had really been up to, out that early in the morning. The one named Gleason had pale red hair, splotchy freckles, and a shifty look; and the other, Gurwitch, stared straight at Cy with beady unblinking eyes. He shook his head hard when Cy asked if they had opened the car. He seemed to be trying to produce a rattle. Whatever those two had really been up to, Keegan was convinced they were telling the truth about finding the car with the bodies of a man and woman.

He turned when Agnes Lamb came to the door and made a little noise. Keegan rose and went into the hall.

"He's here. The man she worked for."

"Did he identify the body?"

"Both of them. She's the manager of his dental clinic. That's why all the stuff in her purse about the place. The man worked at the country club. So he knew them both." Agnes paused a moment. "And he saw them both last night."

Keegan looked at the black woman-cop and tried not to see in her a mere parlay in affirmative action. Horvath thought he was prejudiced. Maybe he was a bit, but he certainly wasn't going to apologize because he thought the world would be a better place if all women were home where they belonged. He sure as hell was never going to be convinced that they made good cops. But he knew Agnes was as good as they come. Black? So what? Keegan didn't pretend to understand blacks all that well, but he supposed Agnes couldn't make head or tail out of him either half the time. Blacks are different from whites in lots of ways. Keegan hoped it wasn't unconstitutional to think so. Hungarians like Horvath were different from Irishmen like himself.

These thoughts came because he couldn't figure out from the way she said it whether Agnes realized what a break this was.

"I put him in your office, okay?"

"I want you there while I talk with him."

Well, you couldn't say that Agnes blushed, but she seemed pleased at this vote of confidence. If women were equal to men Agnes would be as equal as any of them.

Martin Olson stood at the window behind Keegan's desk. The view from there, as Keegan well knew, was the parking lot below and, beyond, Walker Boulevard, leafless trees, a flow of traffic. The dentist turned and, though it was a dull day outside, his eyes did not immediately adjust to the room. He started to come around the desk and bumped into its corner. Agnes took his arm as if to steady him and got him safely into a chair. Facing the window again, Olson looked up at Keegan. There seemed to be tears in his eyes.

Well, it was not a pleasant task to identify two dead bodies. After all, Olson was a dentist, not an M.D.

"The woman is Wanda Wippel?"

Olson nodded. "My God, I can't believe this. Wanda and Georgie!"

"When did you last see them?"

"Last night! I told this officer." Olson gestured vaguely at Agnes, who had taken her station next to the door, a favorite spot of Horvath's when Keegan was interviewing. "I saw them both just last night. They came to my house."

"Together?"

"No, no. Wanda came first. Georgie came later, waking up the whole neighborhood when he did."

"How late was that?"

Olson didn't mean that Georgie had wakened the neighborhood, just that he had brought everyone out of their houses when a watchdog started barking at him.

"I don't blame the animal. Georgie shouldn't have been sneaking around like that. I don't know how he knew Wanda was with me."

"When did she get there?"

Olson looked at the ceiling as he might have glanced at his watch. "It was after eleven when Georgie came. She had been there at least an hour."

"He came to find her?"

Olson glanced at Agnes, opened his hands and studied their palms, looked at Keegan. His mouth was a thin unlipped line as he hesitated. He sighed audibly. "I guess there's no point in not telling you everything."

Everything, as usual, was an incoherent mess. Wanda had worked for Olson for years and years, from the time he opened his clinic. She was a trained surgical nurse but she had been a lot more than that. His voice betrayed emotion as he spoke of the woman and his grief seemed to exceed that of employer for employee. Olson was not married, no. He had never had the time. His life had been the clinic. He could not imagine the place going on without Wanda. He looked apologetic.

"That's a selfish way of looking at it, I know."

"You said Georgie came to your house looking for Wanda. Were they going together?"

"They hadn't been, no. At least to the best of my knowledge. But Georgie had made up his mind he was going to take Wanda out. It was more than that. He wanted to marry her."

"She told you this?"

"She wouldn't have lied, Captain."

"I wasn't suggesting that. Did you know about her and Georgie apart from her telling you?"

"Last night was the first time I ever saw them together."

"He worked at the country club. How did they meet?"

"I might have been responsible for that. I took Wanda to dinner at the club. Georgie was always there. He would have slept there if we had let him. I guess he saw her there and then got in touch with her."

"Had he been taking her out?"

"I'm not sure."

"Why did she come to your house last night?"

"It's ridiculous, but she wanted to talk to me about Georgie. Captain, that is not an area where I can advise anyone. Besides, I didn't want to lose Wanda."

"Was she thinking of marrying him?"

Olson nodded. "I warned her about him."

"What do you mean?"

"I suppose it sounds self-serving. If she didn't marry him she would stay on at the clinic. My motives were mixed. I admit that. But Georgie was a little weird."

"Tell me about it."

If Olson had been genuinely sorrowful when he spoke of his dead administrator, there was impatience and distaste in his tone when he sketched a picture of Georgie. In Olson's description of him, Georgie sounded almost retarded. "No, that's his sister. I think Georgie had all his marbles. Maybe that was the trouble." The dentist's eyes darted to Agnes. "He made a pest of himself where the women members were concerned."

Keegan felt like shutting him off. It wasn't that he didn't want to learn everything he could about the dead man and woman, but Olson was an unlikable man. Very cooperative, but not likable.

"Georgie had a crush on Barbara Rooney," Olson said.

Agnes spoke to that. "What was her reaction?"

Olson seemed to have forgotten that Agnes was behind him. He started and turned to her. "I don't know. I suppose she just dismissed it."

"How did you learn about it?" Agnes went on.

Olson said something, Keegan wasn't listening. Barbara Rooney and Georgie. Wanda and Georgie. Two dead women. And Barbara's death had been made to look like a suicide too, more or less. Keegan was trying to see Barbara Rooney's death in the light of this new information. Georgie. Cy had talked with Georgie when he went out to the country club. If the guy was some kind of sex maniac, falling for someone like Barbara Rooney, being repulsed, he might have...

Keegan shook his head. He had to know a lot more about Georgie before he began constructing explanations like that. But he could not shake off the sense he had that Olson, without knowing he was doing it, had given them their first real break on the Barbara Rooney killing. Keegan didn't like it that a probable suspect was himself dead but that was a whole lot better than not having any suspect at all.

Agnes was all right in trying to get the story out of Olson before the dentist saw the significance of their interest in the connection between Georgie and Barbara Rooney. Except for tangents, like wanting to know how Olson knew of the poem Georgie had written to Barbara Rooney, she kept to essentials. Keegan made notes on what he wanted checked and rechecked in the light of Olson's information.

"I wonder if you'd be willing to let us get all this down on paper, Doctor. Officer Lamb will take you to a room where a record can be made."

"Captain, I'm willing to be all the help I can, but I do have a day's worth of patients waiting for me."

Agnes Lamb said, "I think you'd better call your office and cancel your appointments, Doctor."

Keegan nodded. "She's right, Doctor. We want to know everything you can tell us about Georgie and Barbara Rooney."

Comprehension spread across Olson's face like paint being rolled upon a wall.

"Good God, you don't think that Georgie had something to do with her death too?"

Phil Keegan smiled wisely before he could stop himself. He didn't care what Olson made of it, but he didn't want Agnes Lamb see him playing the big-shot cop with a civilian. It seemed a mark in Agnes Lamb's favor that she ignored it.

25

ROGER DOWLING came along the walk from church to rectory after saying his Mass at noon. Phil Keegan had been there in a pew and Roger had expected him to come into the sacristy afterward. He realized he was disappointed that his old friend had not stopped by. As he knelt on a prie-dieu, saying his thanksgiving after Mass, he had found it difficult to keep out of his thoughts the recent rash of deaths Keegan and his men were investigating. Barbara Rooney's death had been brought to his own doorstep, of course, first by her husband, then by her sister-in-law. Nonetheless these thoughts were a distraction and he successfully drove them away, so successfully that he was ten minutes later than usual when he walked back to the rectory.

"Captain Keegan has already started. I told him to. There is no reason why the whole world should eat reheated soup."

Her tone was not quite accusing. On the one hand, Marie

Murkin approved of priests performing their priestly functions with diligence and that, of course, meant praying for the rest of mankind. On the other hand, she did not like her routine disturbed. But at bottom was her sensible wariness about fanaticism. She did not want the pastor of St. Hilary to become an anchorite. She found it difficult enough to cook for a man who ate anything she set before him; it would be impossible if he fell into the habit of prolonged prayer and forgot about eating entirely.

There was little danger that Phil Keegan would forget about food. He ate as usual with relish and, when he was done, pushed back from the table and looked sternly at Roger Dowling.

"Four people dead, three women, one man. Have you read about the couple found dead in their car?"

"Marie has been keeping me informed."

"Then you know as much as we do."

"Well, let's say Marie does. The little I know only confused me. I mean about the couple. I gather it was carbon monoxide poisoning."

"That is the official finding." Phil tipped his cup and looked into it. "Marie, you got any more coffee out there?

The housekeeper came on the run. It was not in Mrs. Murkin's nature to be docile, but she seemed willing to wait on Captain Keegan hand and foot. Did Phil even notice? Perhaps he was used to having people do his bidding. Poor Marie. Who knew what amorphous hopes filled her dreams of Phil Keegan? She poured his coffee with a wispy little smile on her face.

"Were the ages given on the news for that poor couple correct, Captain?"

"How old did they say they were?"

Marie pretended to remember. Obviously this was a detail that had struck her. "In their forties?"

"That's right. Damned foolishness. People that age parked

in a car by the river, with the motor running; they should have known better."

"Known enough to turn off the motor?" Roger Dowling asked disingenuously. Marie Murkin's lips became a line.

"Maybe they would have frozen to death anyway," Phil said. "Serves them right."

Mrs. Murkin turned on her heel and went back into her kitchen. But surely she would not have been attracted to Phil Keegan at all if he had been a romantic type. It was just his brisk obtuseness that she liked. Her head reappeared in the kitchen door.

"Did you want more coffee, Father?"

Roger Dowling shook his head. He suggested that Phil bring his cup into the study so Marie could clean up. Phil stood, shaking his head, cup to his mouth. When he put it down, he buttoned his jacket.

"That'll have to wait until tonight, Roger." His face clouded. The deaths that had occurred in his jurisdiction did not permit him a half-hour bull session in the study of the St. Hilary rectory during the daylight hours. He might joke about the couple in the car, but Barbara Rooney and Angela Sykes could not be so easily explained. Perhaps the couple in the car presented problems too, if not the romantic ones Marie's interest suggested, then others.

It was a thought Roger Dowling took back into the study where he sat behind his desk and filled a pipe. Surely it was not an easy matter to be asphyxiated in the open air? But that was a technical question, not the sort of question that interested the pastor of St. Hilary's.

A pipeful, half an hour with his breviary, a glance through the latest issue of *The Homiletic and Pastoral Review*, finally settling on a Chesterton. Roger Dowling was not a methodic collector, but he had the better part of the writings of Chesterton, a favorite author since boyhood, and of late he had been rereading the English writer.

Today he opened *What's Wrong With the World?* and was reading it with pleasure when the phone rang. Since this was the time of the house-keeper's nap, Roger Dowling answered it. "This is Father Dowling."

Silence, except for the sound of anxious breathing. Roger Dowling heard the receiver of Marie Murkin's phone lift stealthily.

"Father, I'd like to talk with you."

"Of course."

"Not on the phone." The woman's voice dropped. It sound-ed to Roger Dowling as if she were speaking from a booth, though that might have been due to the slight echo effect of Marie Murkin's open phone.

"You're welcome to come to the rectory. Do you know where it is?"

"What time?"

"Now, if you like."

"I can come tonight. Is eight o'clock all right?"

"Certainly."

"Thank you, Father."

The phone clicked, but before Roger Dowling took the re-ceiver from his ear the voice of Marie Murkin was heard. "You should have got her name."

"Didn't you recognize the voice?" He put down the phone.

He really should not tease Marie like that. She was down-stairs within five minutes, unable to sleep, dying to know the iden-tity of the caller. By then Roger Dowling's denial that he knew could not convince her and she fell into a sullen silence that spoiled the afternoon. A little miffed, repentant, he fled to the school to see how things were going at the parish center.

Mainly what was going on was bridge. There were six tables filled in the old gym and it was clear that the game was being played in earnest. Not even the six dummies looked up when Roger Dowling stopped by. The rooms he passed as he went down the hall contained a group making a quilt, daubers, various other practitioners of arts and crafts. Mainly women, but that was to be expected among the elderly. The parish center was a success, there was no doubt of that, and the reason for it was Edna Hospers.

He found her in the office that had once housed the school principal. That seemed fitting enough. Edna's attitude toward her charges was an odd mixture of adult to children and child to adult. The important thing was that she was not condescending to them. How lucky these old people were to have these quiet years before the end. And in surroundings that assured them that death is not the end after all. Edna looked up with a quizzical smile.

"I've been driven from the rectory."

"Is Marie housecleaning again?"

He let it go. If Marie was out of sorts, it was his fault. He asked Edna to bring him up to date on her work, and she was happy to do so. She lit a cigarette with a filter half the length of it. Smoking was something new with Edna. He wished he had brought his pipe. As he had expected, the center was going as smoothly as it looked.

"We miss Feeney a bit, but that's all."

"You mean you only miss him a bit?"

Laughter and smoke emerged from Edna's mouth. Feeney was a failed experiment. An ex-convict, taken on as a janitor, more or less, who had lived in the school. He was back in Joliet now, a bird returned with relief to his cage. Perhaps they should be looking for a replacement.

"It was good for the others to see someone still more or less active. He wasn't that much younger than they are."

"You should go visit him."

Even before Edna's pained expression, he thought better of the remark. Her husband Gene was in prison for more serious crimes than Feeney had ever dared. This seemed to be Roger Dowling's day to regret what he had said. Not that Edna was petulant in the manner of Marie Murkin. Rather she became if possible more efficient, taking the pastor on a tour of the school. With Edna as guide, Roger Dowling's passage was no longer unobtrusive and soon she left him to himself, or rather with her charges, as he became absorbed in conversations with his aging parishioners. It was nearly five o'clock when he returned to the rectory.

"Didn't Captain Keegan say he was stopping by tonight?" Marie asked after supper.

"I believe he did."

"Don't forget you have a caller."

"Surely you can entertain him until I am free."

"That woman sounded desperate to me."

"Nervous, perhaps. Not desperate. Phil will understand if I am with someone. After all, he isn't paying a formal visit. Or is he?"

"What do you mean?"

"That he doesn't have an appointment," he said quickly. Marie decided not to take further umbrage and Roger Dowling was relieved. He had to stop saying that sort of thing.

Her name was Florence Day, Roger Dowling guessed her to be in her late thirties, and her manner suggested that in other circumstances she would be very much in charge. She was, it emerged, a surgical nurse, head surgical nurse. Mentioning this seemed to restore somewhat her self-confidence.

"Let me say right off that I more or less drew your name out of a hat. Not quite but almost." It seemed important to her not to get it wrong. She looked steadily at Roger Dowling across the desk, her expression that of someone who has witnessed deaths and remarkable feats of surgery and ended with an equivocal view of life. But a view that demanded frankness above all.

"I have heard your name mentioned at the hospital, but to tell you the truth I forget in what connection. But it was a favorable mention, I'm sure of that. There's something I have to talk about and I decided it should be to a minister or a priest and then I remembered your name. So I looked you up and telephoned."

"Then you're not a Catholic?"

"I'm not anything. Religious. I respect it, most of the time, in others. I have seen how much it can mean to people in difficult circumstances. But it is not for me."

"You don't need help?"

"There are many kinds of help."

Roger Dowling nodded. No need to pursue that. He did not think Florence Day had come to talk about her personal religious views or the absence of them.

Florence Day said, "I was a friend of Wanda Wippel. She was found dead in a car parked by the river. There was a man in the car too."

"Yes. George Linger."

"Then you have heard of it. Good." She seemed relieved. She settled back in her chair before she spoke again. "There is something wrong there, Father. I don't know what. Maybe she knew this Linger, as an acquaintance, but the suggestion that she was involved in some tragic affair with him is nonsense. I would have known about it if it were true."

"Wanda Wippel was that close to you?"

"We were close. We were both nurses, that was the connection. Father, if there was a man in Wanda's life his name was not George Linger."

Roger Dowling waited, but when she spoke again, Florence Day's voice had an angry edge.

"There doesn't seem to be any way I can speak of this without sounding like a gossip. But Wanda told me things, I know them whether I want to or not, and what I know may be important now. That's what I want you to help me decide. I can't go down to the police and just babble a lot of things which may do nothing but harm Wanda's name. Not that it makes much difference now to her, but it would to me. I don't want to be telling things I was told in confidence by a friend unless I have to. I'm assuming it doesn't count if I tell you. I mean, it's confidential."

† 171 †

"Yes."

"Other people could be harmed too."

"The man?"

"That bothers me a lot less. I'm not particularly proud of that, but it's true. Theoretically I don't recognize any difference between a man who fools around and a woman who does. But he was taking advantage of Wanda. We talked about that. She thought she could handle him. Women always think they can handle men. And she was determined she was going to marry him."

"Was he married?" There no longer seemed any doubt that Florence Day was unmarried.

"Oh, no. He was too busy making a pile to get interested in women. Wanda worked for him all those years, helping him get rich and when he did decide to get interested in women, of course he looked somewhere else."

"How did she help him get rich?"

"She worked for him! I'm sorry. I don't mean to make it sound so mysterious. I came here to talk about it and it appears that I am. Wanda Wippel worked for a dentist named Martin Olson. She was in love with him. Not an infatuation. This had grown up over the years and was a settled thing in her own mind. She lived in the hope that eventually they would marry. There simply was no other man in her life."

"Olson. Of course. I believe he was the one who identified the bodies."

"He should be getting good at that."

"What do you mean?"

"Do you remember Barbara Rooney, the woman who was killed by an intruder? At least that's the official story. The first indications were that it was suicide but families don't like that verdict and I guess the Rooneys can get what they like."

"What about Barbara Rooney?"

"Olson was in love with her."

"With a married woman?"

For a fleeting moment there was a worldly-wise expression on her face as if she felt Roger Dowling needed instruction in what went on in the moral jungle outside his rectory. She seemed to see the foolishness of that assumption. The foolishness, after all, lay in the story she had come to tell.

"It's the usual thing, I suppose. What's the old phrase? Unrequited love. Wanda loved Martin Olson who loved Barbara Rooney who loved..." Her voice faded away and stopped. When, to finish the thought, she added, "...her husband," Roger Dowling knew that she was aware of Barbara Rooney's reputation for promiscuity.

"What isn't usual is that so many of those involved suddenly die."

"That's right." She moved forward on her chair. "That is what bothers me. So far as I know, and I know I would have known, Wanda had nothing to do with George Linger, if she even knew him. So how can she be involved in an absurd suicide pact with him, like a pair of teen-aged lovers? I just don't believe it."

"Did she ever talk to you of Barbara Rooney's death?"

Florence Day nodded, but it was not in response to Roger Dowling's question. "You see. That is what is bound to happen. I tell you that Wanda was in love with Dr. Olson and that he loved Barbara Rooney and immediately you wonder, did Wanda kill Barbara? Well, she wanted to get Mrs. Rooney out of Dr. Olson's life but murder was not the method she had in mind. We talked about it. I told her temptations are conquered by giving in to them."

"Oscar Wilde."

"He was right. We agreed that Olson would get over her only by getting over her. So to speak. Sorry, nurses talk. Don't think I approve. I don't. Maybe you think the world is going to hell. So do I. But facts are facts. If Barbara Rooney had been as generous with Martin Olson as she was with a lot of others, that most likely would have been the end of it. Wanda was interested in killing his interest in Barbara Rooney, that's all. But would the police agree? They still haven't explained how the Rooney woman died. If I gave them a chance to pin it on Wanda they could then say she took her own life in remorse." She shook her head as if at the folly of police. "I'll tell you one thing. It's a relief to be able to talk about this."

They talked of it for an hour or more. In the course of it, the bell rang and Roger Dowling heard Phil's voice as Marie Murkin admitted him. She took him down the hall to the kitchen and must have closed the door, because at the rare moments when he was not absorbed by the story Florence Day was telling, Roger Dowling could not hear the voices of the housekeeper and the Fox River captain of detectives. What would Florence Day have thought if she knew there was a policeman in the house as she spoke?

26

USUALLY bad news was his stock in trade, but this was surely an exception. No matter how he considered the two bodies found in the car by the riverside it came up bad news for him. What the hell further use would Francis X. Rooney have for Tuttle and Tuttle now that the police had two more bodies on their doorstep? There did not seem to be the remotest hope that Rooney could be linked to the Linger/Wippel deaths. Not even when Peanuts told him that Martin Olson, D.D.S. had identified the bodies.

"The woman worked for him," Peanuts said.

And Georgie worked at the country club, but where did that get Tuttle? The fact was that Peanuts had not been much help before and now he was the bearer of really bad news. Not that Peanuts seemed aware of the import of what he had said. He sat in Tuttle's office, eating a double-dip ice-cream cone, showing no interest at all in Tuttle's reaction. That was good. After all, there was another gruesome possibility, that the Pianones were responsible for all these dead bodies.

Delphine was mad as hell, not that she put it that way. Her fellow religious fanatic Josephine was traveling in a strange crowd and Tuttle would have liked to get a rise out of his secretary but there were more important things at stake. He accepted Delphine's haughty assurance that Josephine did not drink.

"You're absolutely right, Delphine. Find me a bartender who drinks and I'll buy him a drink. Same thing here. But she must have the best vantage point on those who do hang around the Gutter Ball."

"She says you wouldn't believe."

"Like what?"

"The people who come there. Oh, most of them she doesn't know. One nighters, probably from out of town, visiting salesmen, though lots of them stop by whenever they're in town. But that gives you an idea of the level of people. I thought honky-tonk, you know? Jo says not at all, at least not your winos and skid row types. This is the middle class. And above. She knew Barbara Rooney and Angela Sykes."

"No kidding."

Tuttle could imagine the shocked tones of Delphine's informant as his secretary gave him what he already knew, that Angie and Barbara had catted around in the Gutter Ball. Picking up guys. Delphine looked more shocked than disgusted. Tuttle was forever discovering new aspects of Delphine since she got religion. When he first found out about it he worried that it would be bad for business. What had gotten into Delphine? Was she in some kind of trouble? No sign of that. "Don't get me wrong," he said, covering his bets. "I believe in God." This seemed a concession the Almighty ought to appreciate. For Tuttle, God was a faintly malevolent being who could at a whim make Tuttle's life even less successful than it was. Rarely he imagined God as having a special interest in the happy outcome of a Tuttle project. That seemed the case now. Delphine had got religion, met Jo, and thus had a pipeline into the Gutter Ball not even Peanuts could have provided.

"She calls it divine punishment." Delphine did not meet his eye. She was quoting Jo but it was pretty clear she shared the sentiment.

"How does she mean?"

"Think about it. God is not mocked. People keep breaking His commandments, sooner or later they're going to hear from Him." Tuttle squirmed in the booth. He had taken Delphine out to lunch as a way to prime the pump. Not that she had wanted a drink. She must have quit drinking too. And what about smoking? When was the last time he had seen Delphine light a cigarette? Tuttle did not like it. Besides, Delphine's remark seemed to have been directed somehow at him. He did not want to think of life as a process of gaining demerits with a divine scorekeeper. How could he fool someone like that?

"Meaning Barbara Rooney?"

"And Angela Sykes. There's a word for women who behave like that."

"Okay, okay. Did God throw a thunderbolt at them? No. I can't handle the idea of God carving Mrs. Rooney up with a razor blade or driving Angela Sykes into the Fox River."

"He used an instrument," Delphine said, her voice full of disapproval.

"Sure, a razor blade and a two-year-old Volvo."

Delphine just looked at him and Tuttle could have bitten his tongue off. But it was one mistake that turned out to be lucky. She was so goddam mad she just blurted it out.

"No, not a razor or a Volvo. A man."

"And the bartender knows who he is?"

Delphine clammed up but it was too late. Josephine knew or thought she knew the man who had killed Barbara Rooney and

† 177 †

Angela Sykes. He wouldn't be able to get anything more out of Delphine, but what the hell did that matter? He knew where to go to find out whatever it was Delphine knew. So he steered the conversation onto other topics — like how much more Delphine could expect to make with her new responsibilities as president of Ovid Investigations. Religion sure as hell hadn't made Delphine otherworldly. All the while Tuttle was wondering how best he could make use of this new wedge.

He still had not decided when Peanuts sat in his office eating his ice cream cone and telling him about the two bodies. Rooney was off the hook and had no need of the bartender at the Gutter Ball to turn the police away from him. Josephine's claim that she knew the man God had used to strike down two harlots might sound as music of a sort in Rooney's ears.

"Things are a lot quieter at the Gutter Ball lately," Tuttle said.

Peanuts looked uncomprehendingly at him.

"No more murders," Tuttle explained.

Peanuts frowned. God, Tuttle thought, then turned the promising beginning into a prayer. Don't let him tell his uncle. If what the bartender knew was that the Pianones had been responsible for three women and a man dying, Tuttle did not want to hear it. Not only would such knowledge be offensive to Rooney's ears, it would be dangerous for Tuttle to have. Why the hell was life so complicated? Here he had as client one of the premier lawyers of Fox River, a man who had given him a blank check to . . . The nature of the charge was vague. Rooney did not want to be bothered by the cops but what really bothered him was the suggestion that his wife had taken her own life. Would he be satisfied now that the police were adding George Linger and Wanda Wippel to their list of unsolved murders?

"How's Agnes Lamb, Peanuts?"

A sullen expression crept over Peanuts' face; his lower lip

jutted out and he looked at Tuttle out of the corner of his eye, wound-
ed. "That bitch."

"You still going partners with her?"

He knew the answer to that. When Peanuts and Agnes
had gone on patrol together, she insisted on driving. He had had to
invoke the clout of his uncle the councilman to get free of the black
officer. "They got her hanging around the Gutter Ball. They're going to hear from my uncle about that. Bet on it."

"Doing what at the Gutter Ball?"

"Bugging people. Asking questions."

"Maybe she thinks it ain't safe to go there."

"It won't be safe for her."

"What can she learn?"

"Nothing."

The answer came quickly but, though angry, it was untroubled; if the Pianones were worried about anything Agnes Lamb
could find out at the Gutter Ball they had not told Peanuts. She was
bad for business, that was the complaint, because she was a cop,
maybe because she was black.

"It's just routine," Tuttle said. Funny he should have to
explain this to Peanuts. But then it was funny Peanuts was a cop.

27

ONCE SHE got going it had been easy enough talking with Father
Dowling, though Florence Day was not sure what she had accomplished by her visit to St. Hilary's rectory beyond some much needed personal therapy, that is. She had had to talk with someone. So
she had and it had helped, but her basic problem still remained:
should she tell the police of her certainty that Wanda had not been
going out with George Linger? One thing talking with Father Dowling made clear was that she couldn't expect to just say what she
wanted to say and not have others draw conclusions and implications
from it. Martin Olson had apparently lied to the police about Wanda
and George Linger. That was a fact. Because it was a fact that Wanda had loved Olson, not some other man. Florence considered it
certain that Wanda could not have been going out with someone else
without telling her one confidante about it. For Dr. Olson to suggest
that Wanda and the other man were star-crossed lovers invited

speculation as to why he had lied. Florence did not want to enter into such speculation. She just did not want to think about it. If she did she might adopt the fear that Father Dowling had expressed before she left him. Her own life might be in danger.

One of her problems was that her only knowledge of Dr. Olson had come through Wanda, and Florence had never believed the picture that emerged from her friend's romantic portrayals. Florence had reasons to be skeptical of men and their intentions where women were concerned and Wanda was proof positive of why it was so easy for men to get their way with women. If Olson were the paragon Wanda had thought, he would have been unable to lie to the police. But he had lied. Florence felt her skepticism was justified. But she was not afraid of Olson. She feared no man.

Wanda's car was in its appointed stall behind the building. So, too, upstairs her apartment would still contain her furniture and her clothes; her cupboards and refrigerator would be full of the food that Wanda would never eat. What would become of it all? Wanda had no family. For that matter, who would look after funeral arrangements? Florence, parked in her own stall, the motor of her car off, sat there overwhelmed by the sadness of Wanda's death. Her eyes blurred with tears, and she thought that this is the way it would be for herself as well. Who would mourn or miss her when she was gone? What would be the destiny of the possessions she had accumulated? Florence felt, and was, in good physical condition, but she knew from her daily work how quickly health could desert one, how swiftly death came even to the hitherto healthy. It did no good to dismiss these thoughts as morbid. The only way she could avoid them was not to remember Wanda at all.

She pushed open the door of her car and got out. The sun shone but the day seemed more wintry than autumnal. All the branches of the trees were bare now and there was no longer the scent of burning leaves. She rose in the elevator as if she were being lifted above her cares and concerns, but then she thought again of Wanda's now unoccupied apartment.

The following day, at the hospital, the black police officer, Agnes Lamb, came to see her.

"Your name was given us as someone close to the late Wanda Wippel."

"We were friends, yes."

"We're hopeful that you can give us some lead on how to contact her next of kin."

"There isn't any, so far as I know."

The police officer frowned. "Then we have no one to release the body to."

"Who told you I was her friend?"

"Aren't you?" Officer Lamb seemed ready to hear any betrayal.

"I said I was. Who told you?"

She flipped through a notebook but Florence had the feeling she already knew the answer. "The man she worked for. Martin Olson."

Florence nodded. It could hardly have been anyone else. Except perhaps someone in the building where they both had lived. But it seemed that all along she had known it would be Dr. Olson.

"Did you know the deceased's employer?"

Did she have to talk that way just because she was wearing a uniform?

"I knew she worked for him, yes."

"Did you know him?" There was no inflection of impatience, but Florence had the sense that Agnes Lamb would push relentlessly on until her questions were answered.

"I never met him, no."

"How about George Linger?"

"I never met him either. I had no idea he was a friend of Wanda's."

"And the two of you were friends?"

"I can't imagine what she was doing with him."

"She hadn't been acting despondent?"

"No! Just the opposite. She felt that her life was finally becoming what she had wanted."

"Because of George Linger?"

"I told you. I never heard of him from Wanda. I can't believe she knew him."

"Well, she must have known him."

Florence Day said nothing. What was the point? She would sound like a resentful old maid, insisting that her friend had had no man with whom to enter into a suicide pact. The whole thing was crazy. How could she explain why she was so sure Wanda had not killed herself? She just knew it; it wasn't a matter of having proof. But Agnes Lamb hadn't known Wanda, and she was a cop. She wasn't going to record someone else's intuitions in her notebook. Already Florence sensed that Agnes Lamb had come to doubt the claim that Wanda had been a good friend. The notebook closed over the policewoman's finger.

"What will happen to her things?"

"We had to look through the apartment, of course."

"She was very pleased with the way she had furnished it."

"We will continue to try to find next of kin."

"You won't find any."

Agnes Lamb stood. She gave a little shrug at Florence's remark. "Routine."

Florence left the staff lounge with Agnes Lamb and walked her to the elevators. The constant bustle of the hospital swirled around them. The opportunity to tell the police what she had told Father Dowling was past. The notebook had gone into Agnes Lamb's bag. Her intelligent face was receptive as she turned to Florence. Florence could have asked her back to the lounge. There was something else. If the policewoman was told that Wanda had been in love with Martin Olson, not George Linger, she would have something to go on, there would be no need to speculate about the implications of the fact. But Florence feared she had lost what little credibility she had with Agnes Lamb. Now it might do more harm than good to tell her about Wanda and Dr. Olson. In any case, the elevator came, Agnes Lamb stepped in and the doors closed on her farewell nod.

That night at nine when the phone rang Florence hesitated before picking it up as if she already knew who was on the line.

"Is that Florence Day speaking? This is Martin Olson. Dr. Olson. Wanda Wippel worked for me."

"Yes, I know." Florence had closed her eyes when she put the phone to her ear and she kept them closed now, as if the darkness would better enable her to sense the kind of man who was speaking to her.

"Wanda spoke of you a lot. I understand that you were good friends."

Florence nodded. "Yes."

"I told the police that. Have they come to see you?"

"I talked with them this afternoon."

"I'm sorry about that, but I felt I should tell them everything I could, anything that might help them."

"I wasn't of much help."

"There is something. I understand that Wanda has no family at all. I knew she had no immediate family but the police have been unable to locate even remote relatives. Did Wanda ever mention anyone to you?"

"I don't think there are any. I told the police that."

Olson seemed to hum into the phone for a moment. "Someone will have to take charge. We can't have her buried as a pauper. You and I seem to be the only people who knew her at all well."

"That's right."

"Now that Georgie Linger's dead," he added.

"Who in the world is George Linger anyway?"

There was a pause. "Surely the police must have told you if you didn't read it in the paper. They were found together in the car."

"I know that. But she never mentioned his name to me."

"Really? Well, perhaps that isn't very surprising. My impression was that she was not terribly proud of the liaison. It started on his side, you should know that. Maybe Wanda did not know how to handle a persistent male. But it became something else."

"She discussed it with you?"

The pause was brief but she could almost hear his thoughts shuffle. "Not intentionally. It came out, in bits and pieces, you know."

"That doesn't sound like Wanda to me. I had absolutely no inkling that George Linger existed."

"That is surprising. Wanda was quite definite about your friendship. She admired you a good deal."

Was he waiting for her to return the compliment? Wanda idolized you, Doctor. She thought you were exactly the man she had dreamed of since she was a girl.

He said, "I wondered if you and I might not take charge of Wanda's funeral. Of course I will cover the expenses, but someone should go speak with the funeral director, that sort of thing."

Florence was flooded with contradictory emotions. Her first reaction was: how good of him to do this. But that was immediately followed by other thoughts, other feelings. Could a man who did this have wanted to harm Wanda, her reputation, herself? My God, how wrong about him she must be. And to think she had thought of going to the police in order to turn their attention to Martin Olson. She regretted now having spoken with Father Dowling and knew a fleeting fear that he would pass on what she had said to someone else. But she had trusted him when he said their conversation was confidential. It would not go beyond him. And thank God for that. She had opened her eyes convinced that the voice that spoke to her over the phone was that of a compassionate and caring man. Exactly the man Wanda had always claimed he was. Florence was ashamed of her skepticism.

"She was a very nice person," he was saying. "I shall miss her very much. Would you share this responsibility with me?"

"Yes! Yes, of course. I would be proud to."

"I knew you would." And he did sound as if he had never doubted it. "I have told the police that they can release the body in my name. As for a funeral director, I thought of Hennessy. Do you agree?"

"I don't know a thing about it."

"I've heard good things of him."

"Whatever you say."

"When can we get together, Florence? You don't mind if I call you Florence, I hope?"

It was as Florence and Martin that they continued the conversation. They arranged to meet the following day. He would pick her up at her apartment at six-thirty. After they consulted Hennessy they could have dinner together.

28

JOSEPHINE felt the same awed satisfaction she felt when the Reverend Seely explained some especially snarled text from Revelations. Everything fell into place. One with eyes to see could see as plain as day. God had used his instrument again. Jo did not know what iniquity the couple found dead in the car by the river had been guilty of but she had no doubt that God had smitten them with good reason. That seemed clear from the instrument.

She read the story in the paper. The woman had worked for a Dr. Olson. Some publicity for him. The woman must have been up to something with the man found dead with her. And they had been punished. Of course that was not the way those who talked it over at the bar of the Gutter Ball saw it.

The prevailing view was that it had been an accident, not suicide. The couple had parked and were going at it hot and heavy with the motor running and that was it. Jo pointed out that the newspaper account did not suggest that. Both bodies were fully clothed. Her remark drew tolerant smiles. Did she expect to have it all spelled out in the newspaper? She had to read between the lines.

Well, she read between the lines all right, and she found a very different message, a message those carousing in the Gutter Ball would be well to take to heart. But they had not been taught to flee from the wrath that was to come. She and Delphine had seen eye to eye on that and no wonder.

When Jo first saw the face familiar to her from the Tabernacle, she had wanted to hide. She must not be seen in here, behind the bar, by someone who would recognize her from Reverend Seely's Tabernacle. But then she wondered what the other woman was doing, and that turned the tables. She would be able to watch and see if the woman misbehaved. If there was a backslider here it was not Josephine.

Well, it wasn't the other woman either. Delphine, as her name turned out to be. Their eyes met through the clouds of cigarette smoke and Jo knew the recognition was mutual. The other woman was not embarrassed. She held Jo's gaze and dipped her head in the direction of the Ladies'. Jo nodded, indicating she understood, and as soon as she could get away she met the woman in the john. The business card really hit her. Ovid Investigations?

"Are you a detective?"

"I've seen you at the Tabernacle."

Jo nodded. "I recognized you right away."

"I'm a private detective. Look, I have to talk with you, but this isn't the place for it. How late do you work?"

"Three."

"In the morning?" Delphine could not conceal her surprise.

"It's my shift. I'm not exactly proud of working here."

"I know what you mean. Can we get together tomorrow? What time do you get up?"

Sometimes Jo slept till noon, but that was rare. She was

usually up and going before ten o'clock. Delphine said she would drop by the apartment at ten the next morning.

Jo was up and ready by nine o'clock but Delphine did not come until nearly ten-thirty so there went some extra sleep she could have used. Delphine was apologetic about being late and this, plus seeing her now at home and not at the Gutter Ball, put Jo at an advantage. She had been thinking of what she would tell Delphine. If the woman wasn't a private detective Jo would have been inclined to tell her the whole thing, what God was doing to punish those who hang around the Gutter Ball. They could have talked with the ease of two people who had been saved at Reverend Seely's Tabernacle. But Delphine was a detective and that made a difference. So she made up her mind to let Delphine start the conversation. When she did it was all about Reverend Seely.

"How did you happen to go there?"

"I saw him on television."

"Me too! The first time I saw him in person I was sort of disappointed. I might not have gone back but I watched him on TV some more and then wanted to take another look at him. That second time, it was completely different."

"For me the first time did it," Jo said. "I suppose you wonder why I keep on working where I do after being saved."

"And you must wonder about what I do."

"How come you showed up at the Gutter Ball?"

"Believe me, it was on business."

Her business brought them right to what Jo would have wanted to tell her about, the deaths of Barbara Rooney and Angela Sykes.

"There seems to be a connection between the Gutter Ball and their deaths. Each of them spent their last night alive at the bar."

"Who are you working for?"

"A lawyer named Tuttle."

"Does he go to the Tabernacle with you?"

Delphine's laughter was a lot like the laughter Jo heard every night at the Gutter Ball. "You'd have to know Tuttle to see how funny that question is."

"Why is he interested in those deaths?"

"He represents Mr. Rooney, the man whose wife was killed."

"So you tell what you learn to Tuttle and he tells her husband?"

"That's the way it's *supposed* to go."

Delphine was waiting. Jo found that she trusted the woman.

"I would talk to you but I don't want what I say passed on to other people."

"Why not?"

"You'd understand if I told you."

"That sounds as if you know who killed those women."

"Can just the two of us talk?"

Delphine was clearly torn in two directions. Curiosity, of course, and maybe the temptation to lie. But she didn't.

"If I find out something that would be helpful to Tuttle I can't promise I won't tell him."

"I don't think you'll want to tell him. Not if he's the kind of person you suggested."

"Maybe not."

Jo took that as assurance enough. She had not realized how desperate she was to tell someone what she had seen happening right before her eyes at the Gutter Ball.

"God struck those women down," Jo said solemnly. "They flaunted His law and finally He slew them."

She saw the doubt flicker in Delphine's eyes, sparkle, and then go out. Here was a listener who had been saved and knew what the score was. "God used the same instrument both times."

"Tell me about it."

"I don't know his name. It didn't seem important that I try to find out. He was in the bar the night before I read about Mrs. Rooney in the paper. And the night Angie drowned I saw him hiding in her car in the parking lot."

"You don't have any idea who the man is?"

"He is only an instrument."

"But you would recognize him again?"

"What difference would it make?"

"What if he wasn't acting for God?"

"You wouldn't say that if you had known those women. They were calling down the divine wrath on their heads."

Delphine nodded. "I can see that that would be possible. But can we be sure? What if he is just a murderer. Would God want him to go unpunished?"

"He didn't want those women to go unpunished."

"Those who killed the martyrs were acting as God's instruments, weren't they?"

"The martyrs were innocent."

Jo poured them both a cup of coffee. This was the kind of conversation she loved and did not have much opportunity for. To seek and find the hidden hand of God in the affairs of men was an exciting thing. Life could seem so meaningless, just a flow of events, but looked at as God's plan its meaning was sometimes divulged. Jo had no doubt that her interpretation of the way Barbara Rooney and Angela Sykes had died was the right one.

"I wonder if Reverend Seely would agree with you?"

"Of course he would."

"Did you tell him about it?"

"No."

The admission seemed to transfer the advantage to Delphine.

"It would be awful to be wrong about something like that."

† 191 †

"I don't think I'm wrong."

"I can see that. I hope you aren't. But I wish you'd let Reverend Seely decide the matter."

Jo could not think of a convincing answer to that. Reverend Seely had a good deal more experience than she had in reading the meaning of events. His sermons on Afghanistan and Poland had been marvelous. Next to such global events the death of two women would be child's play for him. Nonetheless, she found that she did not like to have her judgment questioned. But that was pride. Delphine was right. She could be mistaken, and if she was, a man who should be punished was walking around scot-free.

The upshot of her morning coffee with Delphine was that Jo agreed to consult Reverend Seely on the matter. Delphine asked if she would abide by his decision and Jo just looked at her. That went without saying, as Delphine should have known. Still, she was surprised when Delphine insisted that they go immediately to the Tabernacle and consult Reverend Seely.

"Why wait? If that man is to be treated as a murderer, we don't want to waste any time."

There was no good answer to that either so far as Jo could see. By eleven o'clock they were on their way to the Tabernacle in Delphine's car.

29

THE CONCERN that had been in her voice when she spoke to him in the rectory was absent from Florence Day's voice when she telephoned Roger Dowling to inquire about funeral arrangements for Wanda Wippel. Here was no worried woman, but a friend intent on doing a last kindness to the departed.

"You're taking care of things?"

"The police have tried to find a relative but they can't. I'm not surprised. Wanda would surely have mentioned them if there were any. I think she was content to be quite alone, without ties."

"That sounds very sad. But of course you were her friend."

"She was alone but not lonely," Florence Day said and Father Dowling felt that she might be describing herself. "Father, I really don't know how to arrange a funeral. I am hoping that you will advise us."

"Us?"

"Dr. Olson and I are taking joint responsibility. Not financially. He is taking care of all expenses. He feels indebted to Wanda and this is his way of showing it."

"That sounds very generous," Roger Dowling said carefully. He waited a moment but no further explanation was forthcoming. "The two of you seem to have been all she had by way of a family."

"It seems so little to do."

Roger Dowling found it difficult to believe that she had completely forgotten her animus against Wanda Wippel's employer. Yesterday, right here in this study, she had as much as accused Dr. Olson of doing away with his executive manager.

"First you must select a funeral director."

"That will be Hennessy."

"A good choice."

"Dr. Olson chose him. Does he do everything?"

"That depends on what you mean by everything."

"I would like you to take part, Father."

"Of course. Was Wanda a Catholic?"

"Does that matter?"

"Not to my taking part, no. But it would affect what I might do."

"She wasn't a Catholic. She did believe in God. We talked about it, the way people do. She believed."

He did not blame Florence Day for making it sound as though God had been honored by this acknowledgment. Perhaps we all sound presumptuous when we speak about God, as if He depended on us rather than the reverse. It seemed odd that Florence Day should have plucked his name from a hat when she was looking for an adviser and should come to him again when she seemed to have made a 180 degree turn so far as her attitude toward Dr. Olson was concerned. There was of course another possibility. He knew of her suspicions. If she no longer referred to them, she could be counting on his remembering. It was a species of insurance.

"Did you propose this arrangement to Dr. Olson?"

"No. He got in touch with me."

"So you finally met him."

"This was on the phone."

"Haven't you met him yet?"

"We will get together later today. I wanted to speak to you first so I could tell him I had taken care of the religious side. Having already talked with you, I felt it was one contribution I could make."

"So you'll see him later today?" His eyes drifted to the electric clock which sat on one of the shelves of the far bookcase; its hum was audible but he seldom noticed it. It was five after ten in the morning.

"Actually, this evening. We'll go to Hennessy's and then have dinner together."

The last remark was made with an edge to her voice and he got what he took to be her meaning. She wanted no comment on her turnabout. She must know she was giving the appearance of stepping swiftly into Wanda Wippel's shoes. Roger Dowling took the conversation back to what she wanted him to do. They settled on a ceremony at the funeral home, some readings from Scripture, a word or two from him. Yes, he would come on to the cemetery for the burial. He felt he was being asked to be a prop, perhaps one that clashed with the setting. What would Nancy Rooney say of his participation in so ecumenical a service? It would be less ecumenical than non-denominational. But Roger Dowling had no compunction in calling down God's mercy and blessing on the soul of Wanda Wippel.

After he hung up he did a few pastoral chores, principal among them making out copies of baptismal certificates to send to three former parishioners who were going to marry. He said several hours of his breviary but put it down when he found he did not want to set aside the thoughts that oppressed him.

It was the notion that Florence was taking Wanda's place with Dr. Olson that, in the light of what Florence had come to tell him yesterday, filled him with something very much like foreboding. The oral surgeon's appearance, if only on the edges, of the lives of Barbara Rooney and Angela Sykes was difficult to ignore now that he appeared again in the foreground of the Wippel and Linger deaths. Four deaths, all of them carrying an unconvincing suggestion of suicide, all of them involving in some way Martin Olson. But surely there were others who figured in the same more or less peripheral way in those deaths? Francis X. Rooney, for example. He had known Angela Sykes, his wife had been a patient of Olson, and thus he was indirectly connected with Wanda Wippel. And what of his sister Nancy? Thought of in the abstract, she could be said to have motives for wanting to kill her sister-in-law, and that motive might have extended to Angela Sykes as well. It wasn't just that he had no way to tie her to Wanda and George Linger. He found it difficult to imagine her killing one person, let alone four. Was his ability to feel otherwise about Martin Olson due to the fact that he had never met the man? Just talking to him on the phone seemed to alter Florence Day's ability to think of him as possibly responsible for the death of Wanda.

When he went into the kitchen Marie Murkin was not there. He stood at the back door and looked out at the overcast autumnal day. The fallen leaves had lost their brilliance and it was impossible to ignore the coming on of winter. Marie came up the basement stairs, entered the kitchen, and sighed. She was an indefatigable worker but nonetheless liked to dramatize her labors. Roger Dowling found it best to ignore these signals of Herculean toil. She knew he thought the world of her as a housekeeper and there was no need to keep telling her so.

"Is Dr. Olson a good dentist?"

She finished pouring herself a cup of coffee, then looked at him. "Toothache?"

"No, no. It's just a question. I remember you went to him last year."

"If you need a regular dentist you can't go to him. He is a surgeon. His patients are referred to him by regular dentists."

"What kind of man is he?"

"My regular dentist is Lipton. Would you like me to make an appointment for you?"

"You know I go to Hogan."

"Then why are you asking about other dentists?"

"I asked about Dr. Olson. Tell me about him."

"What's to tell? He's a dentist. Most of the time I saw his face upside down while he was working on me. It's the nurses you really see at a place like that. They get you ready and then the great man sweeps in and does his work and disappears."

"Did you meet a woman named Wanda Wippel?"

"Ah." Mrs. Murkin sat at the kitchen table, her coffee mug squarely before her and a knowing smile on her face. "I thought so. The woman found dead in lover's lane."

"That's a pretty lurid way of putting it, Marie."

"A suicide pact with her lover. I'm just repeating what the newspaper as much as said."

"Did she strike you as a doomed and tragic figure?"

"Ha. Talk about a Nazi. She ran that clinic like a military camp. By the numbers. When she spoke the rest of them jumped. I wonder what will happen to the place now she's gone."

"Olson was that dependent on her?"

Marie looked wise. "I got the impression from the nurses — nothing they said, just the way they acted — that they thought there was something going on between Miss Wippel and the doctor."

"Really?" Roger Dowling felt bad to encourage Marie Murkin to gossip — not that she needed much external stimulus to do so — but he did want her impressions of Dr. Olson's clinic. Besides, he knew that Mrs. Murkin's conscience was numb in this area. She had even developed a little theory about her gossiping. She was his eyes and ears in the parish; a pastor should know what is going on and he should be glad that she just happened on as much news as she did. She was certainly an observant witness of any surroundings she found herself in.

"I would guess that if there was anything going on it was only in Miss Wippel's mind. I suppose it seemed coming to her. If she ran the doctor during the day, why shouldn't she have full-time control of him?"

"Not a very romantic view."

"You would have had to know her. And him."

"What were your impressions of him?"

Marie Murkin sipped her coffee and studied Roger Dowling. Since he usually stopped her when she wanted to tell him things, she was suspicious of his interest now. But she had already satisfied herself as to the reason for his interest.

"He didn't kill her," Marie Murkin said, putting down her mug.

"Good grief, was that your impression of him, that he was unlikely to kill the woman who ran his clinic like a military camp?"

"No, but I know what you're getting at. The only thing there was is what I've said. She probably had a crush on him. Have Captain Keegan check with the other nurses."

"Phil Keegan is not the least bit curious about Dr. Olson's clinic so far as I know."

She wrinkled one corner of her mouth into a skeptical smile. "But I'm sure they'll tell him too that it was all on her side. He is a good surgeon but apart from that a kind of mechanical man. Apparently his whole life is dentistry. He has no family, just the clinic. And he chatters in the silliest way when he is operating. No, he didn't do it."

"Well, that's good to hear."

"You're being sarcastic. Why doesn't Captain Keegan ask me these things directly?"

There seemed little point in trying to dissuade her on that

point. If he did try, she would be more convinced than ever that he was acting for Phil Keegan in putting these questions. But he made a try.

"Olson and the woman who was here yesterday, Florence Day, are taking care of funeral arrangements for Wanda Wippel."

"Is that why she called?"

Marie had answered the kitchen phone and then buzzed him in his study when Florence telephoned.

"That's right."

"Don't tell me Miss Wippel was a Catholic."

"Many military people are."

She made a face. "Will you bury her from Saint Hilary's?"

He shook his head. "She wasn't a Catholic. There'll be a little service at the funeral home."

Marie Murkin held her tongue. She felt as Roger Dowling presumed Nancy Rooney would about his doing something like that. Marie Murkin agreed that God loves everybody but she was equally certain He loves more those who love Him back. She was not tolerant of the view that people could change at the end of their lives, getting religion belatedly and ending up with a harp. Roger Dowling had learned that it did little good to remind her of the parable of the workers. Nor did he want her to get going on Frank Sinatra again.

Back in his study, he looked up the address of Dr. Olson's clinic in the phone book. After he had said Mass and had lunch, he would drop by the clinic.

30

IT IS ODD how the past lies hidden in the present. Sometimes, replacing a crown, when he removed the old one and laid bare the evidence of work done long ago, perhaps by a dentist now dead, Martin Olson imagined some future colleague examining his own work. It seemed to connect things in a way he was unable to express. People talked about immortality. Well, we live in our work. He would be around for a long time, in porcelain and silver and gold, in the mouths of his patients.

These were strangely meditative thoughts for an oral surgeon, but such thoughts assailed him lately. And images, memories, the past again. It is all there, encoded in the brain cells, liable to come out at any time, causing that dizzying sensation that the past was present as another room is present. When he was a kid, once at his cousins', playing hide and go seek in the huge house in which they lived, he had hidden under a bed in an upstairs room, lying there listening to the voices of the others as they tried to find him. He could feel now the delicious excited anxiety with which he lay waiting to be caught. Of course he would be caught. It was only a matter of time. But for those few moments he lay concealed, waiting, knowing discovery would come, yet yelping with surprise when the others came upon him. How soon would his hiding place be discovered now?

Introspection was an upsetting activity after years, a lifetime really, of living in his actions, his whole attention focused outside himself. It was like seeing himself from outside and from within at the same time. That thought could be so absorbing was a surprise. He sat in his office in the clinic, behind him the difficult work of his day — he performed his operations as early as he could persuade patients to come — and, without Wanda to organize the rest of his day, he felt uncharacteristically free. There would have been no escape from thought even if he had wanted it, but he didn't. He liked it. Maybe this is what that pathetic Georgie did in his little nest behind the locker room at the club. Georgie. Wanda. Angie and Barbara. All dead. He formed the words in his mind but they did not seem enough to say what had happened. Words are used all the time for such ordinary purposes and do not seem up to the job of saying that some human being has stopped existing. Has been killed. Murdered. Those words formed in his head, words he had known all his life, and which now tried to take on a serious job for the first time. And I am a murderer, he thought. That was the most incredible sentence of all. Not that he doubted its truth. He wasn't crazy. He knew what he had done. He had done it deliberately and carefully and at the time it had seemed the most reasonable thing in the world. Kill Barbara, kill Angie. And then Georgie and Wanda. It was like algebra. Given one thing, other things followed; they couldn't be resisted. And the line did not stop with Georgie and Wanda. Now there was Florence Day.

What had been happening was so obvious that he could

not believe the police had not picked up the thread and followed it to his door. The confusing scene at the Rooneys produced in concert with the ghost of his father who seemed to lurk in his genes might have been the product of his more rational self alone. The sequence of killings had a logic that appealed to his developed personality. After Barbara, Angie, and then Wanda and Georgie. And now Florence Day. No one could question the inference that led him onward.

Wanda had mentioned Florence; Florence was the only person Wanda ever mentioned, giving some suggestion of a life apart from the clinic. He could imagine Wanda talking freely to Florence as he himself talked freely to Wanda. A confidant is necessary. A person has to let the words out of his head from time to time or it will explode. Thus he had become convinced that Wanda had confided in Florence Day her love for Martin Olson and her settled intention to marry him. She had told him this eventually and he found he had always somehow known it. Florence Day could have known it that way too, even if Wanda had not said anything, but Martin Olson would bet that she had spoken of it to the one person she did speak to. He was going to bet Florence Day's life on it.

Florence's knowledge put him in jeopardy, yet he did not deny he felt as he had hiding beneath that bed years ago. He would be caught. The police could not possibly fail to see that he was the explanation of these four deaths. That certitude did waver, however.

The deaths of Wanda and Georgie were still ascribed to causes unknown. Oh, there was no doubt that they had died of carbon monoxide poisoning. And it did look as if they were lovers who had decided to exit the world together. What could not be seen was the fact that Wanda had helped him subdue Georgie. She had actually given him the Novocain injection and driven the car with Georgie beside her to the river. Olson rode in the back seat much as he had with Angela. Wanda took instructions as she always had. Take a left, pull over here, leave the motor running. Had she suspected anything before the needle slipped into the flesh behind her ear?

The thought that he was going to get away with killing these people both pleased and displeased him. Not to be caught would be like lying forever under that bed without being discovered. What was the point of hiding if it meant you would be hidden forever? But if he were caught now the consequences were unthinkable. He would lose his clinic, his freedom, everything.

Everything. His life came down to things. This office, this building, his Porsche, his house. Anything that money could buy came within the range of his desire. What would he be without them? Already he was beginning to see how hard it was going to be to run the clinic without Wanda. She had certainly not been training anyone to take over for her. Why should she have? But he did not want to think of that now. For months things would go on as a result of her organization: the appointments had been made, everyone would know what to do. And after? He would face that when he came to it. If he came to it. For the moment things were tenuous. Even the buzz of his phone seemed indecisive. He picked it up. The police were on the line. He punched the button and said hello.

"The body of Wanda Wippel has been released to Hennessy Funeral Home," Officer Lamb told him, after identifying herself. "I understand you'll take over from here."

"That's right. Has there been any final word on what happened?"

"Accidental death due to carbon monoxide poisoning."

"Such a shame. Florence Day and I will be making the arrangements. She was a friend of Wanda's."

"We're still unable to discover any relatives."

"Thank you for calling, Officer."

He put the phone carefully into its cradle. The childrens' voices were excited as they searched for him in the other rooms but now they grew fainter, they were giving up, going downstairs. He had won, he had won. Why did he feel he had lost?

For lunch he had yogurt from the little refrigerator in his

office. The afternoon would be a busy one but that did not explain his meager meal. He almost never ate lunch. He had to fast in order to keep trim. But he liked this time to himself in his office. Wanda had gone out to lunch so he had been free of her as well. It was a comfortable office. He had furnished it on the model of an advertisement he had torn from an airline's magazine on one of his trips to Acapulco. An ad for bourbon pictured a well-groomed executive leaning back against his desk, a glass of honey-colored liquor in his hand. The office seemed to Martin Olson the essence of achievement. He sat in that very office now, holding yogurt rather than bourbon. The wallpaper had finally been impossible to match, though Wanda had pursued the matter for months, writing the magazine, the advertising agency, finally the wallpaper company. It was a discontinued line. They had something else like it, very close. It was close enough, but only close, and it took some of the pleasure out of sitting in the room. He still had the page from the magazine and from time to time he got it out and looked around the room, verifying that he had duplicated the setting in which the man advertised bourbon. It was like stepping into the world contained in the glossy pages with their impossibly perfect photography, pages where the pursuit of things was understood to be the meaning of life.

There were a surprising number of cancellations early in the afternoon and Martin Olson did not like the tone in the receptionist's voice when she told him. She seemed to think she was the character in the horror movie who first expresses the thought that eerie things are happening. As if the cancellations were connected with Wanda's death, the clinic under a hex because of it. He wondered if many patients would show up for Wanda's services. She had not been liked, Wanda, but she had been respected. Besides, the circumstances of her death could bring out the curious. With the cancellations he had more time to think, and he did not welcome it. He was tired of thought. That is why, when he was buzzed and told that Roger Dowling had come to see him, Martin Olson was almost happy.

"*Father* Dowling," the receptionist repeated significantly.

Priest? And then he thought of Wanda's funeral. "I'll come out."

A little courtesy to the priest, go to meet him in the lobby and bring him to the office.

As soon as he came into the hallway and pulled his door shut, Martin Olson could see the priest. Dowling stood in the lobby, thin, somewhat stooped in profile. His lean face reminded Martin Olson of someone, he did not know who. The black suit and Roman collar seemed just the clothing for Roger Dowling. When the priest turned at his greeting, Martin Olson was struck by the eyes. Just so his cousins had looked when they peered beneath the bed and found him hiding there.

They shook hands and Martin Olson led the way back down the hallway to his office.

"Florence Day came to see me," Father Dowling said when they were seated. The priest looked around the office but the waited-for remark did not come. Olson was prepared to get the conversation going with the story of how he had come to furnish his office, but perhaps it was best to go right to the funeral. After all, that was the priest's only interest. Fanciful thoughts about the man of God seeing through to one's soul were just that, fanciful, and he had best not indulge in them.

"I thought we might talk a bit about what I will do."

"Whatever you think proper, Father. You're the expert. I put everything in your hands."

"Was Wanda a religious person?"

He should have been prepared for the question, but he wasn't. He realized he didn't even understand what the question meant. He said that to Father Dowling.

"I suppose it does mean many things. Do you know if she believed in God?"

Olson laughed. "This is a pretty busy place, Father. We don't normally have time to discuss such matters." The priest smiled.

"I suppose not. I thought you might have talked about such matters elsewhere."

"Miss Wippel worked for me, Father."

"Yes. I understood she was at your home the night she died."

"That's right. Not a social call, however. How much do you know about the circumstances of her death?"

"Not as much as I'd like to. Why did she come to you that night?"

"It concerned Georgie. The man she was found with. Linger."

"Yes, I've heard the name. He was employed at your club?"

"At the country club, yes."

"You knew him, then?"

"Oh, yes. All the members know Georgie."

"But he gave you a poem he had written, I understand."

Olson hoped his smile did not waver. He did not like the relentless if quiet way Dowling put his questions. "How did you ever hear of that?"

"I have friends on the police force."

"And I'm telling you what happened to Wanda and Georgie? You must know far more than I do. The deaths have been ruled accidental, by the way. I had a call just before you came. I suppose that's a merciful ruling."

"You think it's false?"

Olson hesitated before speaking. "Let's say I'd be surprised if it's true. Wanda came to me because Georgie was, well, pretty insistent in his pursuit of her."

"Where would they have met?"

"I must take the blame for that, I'm afraid. I took Wanda to the club..."

Dowling's brows rose slightly and no wonder. Olson had

just denied seeing Wanda socially. He decided it was best not to explain. "Georgie apparently got a look at her and that was the beginning."

"Was she very beautiful?"

"Georgie must have found her so."

"Did he write a poem for her?"

"Not that I know of."

"The poem he did write was to Barbara Rooney, I understand."

"Well, it was about her."

"Why did he give it to you?"

"I took it."

"Did you really?"

"Imagine, a pro shop bum writing love poetry to one of the members."

"I had been developing a theory, Doctor. About the deaths of Mrs. Rooney and Angela Sykes. When I heard about the poem, I thought, of course, that's it. Some spurned lover has taken his revenge. It's just as you say. Not only was he smitten by a married woman, he was her social inferior. He had no hope. Perhaps she was amused when he revealed his love. Enraged, he killed her."

"That sounds plausible." Was this the line the police had been pursuing? Olson felt a sharp twinge of regret for having included Georgie in Wanda's exit. Georgie. Of course!

Father Dowling said, "There had to be a connection between someone and those two women. Of course there are other possibilities."

"Georgie could be the one. That may be the reason for his suicide."

"I thought the deaths were accidental."

"That's the official verdict. I think most people will see what happened."

"Will they? I don't. A woman who came to you to complain

about Georgie then drove off and committed suicide with him. There again, Georgie could have been the explanation, but he, alas, is dead."

"Father, I think you've hit on something. And Georgie's being dead doesn't change a thing." Olson rotated back and forth in his leather chair, a thoughtful expression on his face. "Maybe only Georgie committed suicide. It doesn't make sense that Wanda would. She wasn't the type and even if she had been, a pact with Georgie was the last thing she would have entered into. Try this. Georgie is spurned a second time. That's too much. Wanda is going to get what Barbara Rooney got. By now, however, self-disgust was almost as strong as his anger and, after he killed Wanda, he killed himself."

Father Dowling, the tips of his fingers touching almost prayerlike under his nose, nodded and smiled. "Very good. Extremely good." But his smile gave way to a frown. He shook his head. "No. No, there's a flaw. There was no sign of a struggle in the car. Death was due to carbon monoxide poisoning."

"Of course. That's how he killed her."

"But she would not have sat there without a struggle."

"She was already unconscious."

"Knocked out?" Dowling shook his head. "There's no sign of that."

"There are lots of ways to render a person unconscious."

"Yes, I suppose you're right. On that subject you would be an expert. What kind of anesthetic do you use here, Doctor?"

Olson looked at the priest. "It doesn't matter. Georgie would not have had access to them."

"No. Let's forget about Georgie. Who else could have been connected with all the people who have died?"

Olson looked at his watch. "You didn't come here to play guessing games, Father."

"It's no longer a guessing game. What method did you use, injections, pills, what?"

Boo. Dowling had looked beneath the bed and found him. Olson said nothing.

"That is characteristic of all four deaths, the absence of a struggle. Why did Barbara Rooney submit so docilely to the slashing of her wrists? I suppose Angela Sykes was knocked out when she went into the river in her car. Did you drive those two inert people to the river and leave them there with the motor running? How did you get back?"

Olson got up, went to the door, and locked it. He looked down at Father Dowling.

"Let's stop guessing."

"I already have. Sit down, Doctor. You are not going to harm me. It would do you no good. You have embarked on an endless series. You cannot kill enough people to cover up your first terrible deed. You were infatuated with Barbara Rooney, I suppose."

"I loved her." He did sit down. As with Wanda, he would take advantage of the opportunity to speak of what he had done.

"Ah. No wonder you were so incensed by Georgie's attentions. But why did you kill her?"

"You wouldn't understand. You're a priest." He said it with a sneer.

"And unmarried? You never married, did you, Doctor?"

"That's different."

"Tell me about Barbara Rooney."

Olson repressed the rage he felt. He began to nod and his shoulders slumped as he sought an attitude of remorse, whatever it was the priest expected.

"Not here, Father. Let's go into the room next door."

"What's wrong with this office?"

Olson unlocked the door. This seemed to reassure Dowling. Turning the lock had been a threatening act; now it was undone.

"I feel more comfortable where I usually deal with patients."

"I am not a patient."

Olson smiled as at a joke. He went down the hall and into the next room. The hypodermic needle was on the little table next to the dental chair. He had it in his hand before the priest followed him into the room. The prick of the needle surprised Dowling but the only noise he made was a sharp inhalation. Olson's thumb depressed the plunger and Dowling's eyes rolled out of sight. The anesthetic did not take effect that quickly. Obviously Dowling was not someone who took shots easily.

Olson caught the priest beneath an elbow and guided his rubbery-legged victim to the dental chair, where the injection would soon take over from Dowling's fainting spell.

31

AGNES LAMB took the call and then came in to tell him what she had done. Keegan tried to keep impatience out of his voice.

"You asked Tuttle's secretary and the Reverend Seely to come down and see me?"

"That's right. And Josephine, the bartender at the Gutter Ball, will be coming too."

"Fine, fine. The more the merrier. Is Seely going to consult the Bible and come up with the explanation of the Rooney and Sykes deaths?"

"I think the two women will do that. They consulted him and he advised them to call us."

Keegan shut up. He had caught a minute or two of Seely's program and watched the healings and the preaching. Seely looked like a dude in his pastel double-knit suits and his hair all teased and sprayed. An actor. Keegan didn't know what the explanation of those healings was. It wasn't that he did not believe in miracles, he did, but he did not think the Lord would choose someone like Seely for His instrument or turn it into a TV extravaganza ending up with a pitch for donations. For all he knew Agnes Lamb went to Seely's Tabernacle and he did not want to give her further reason for thinking that he did not take her seriously. But why the hell was Tuttle's secretary and a bartender from the Gutter Ball going to Reverend Seely for advice? Anyone connected with Tuttle was not to be trusted. Keegan could say that aloud to Agnes Lamb.

"Like Mr. Francis X. Rooney?"

"That's different."

Agnes smiled. Keegan looked away. He didn't blame her. Still, it was different, Rooney and Delphine. Delphine worked for that little shyster.

"Tuttle isn't coming, is he?"

"They didn't mention him."

"If he shows up, keep him out."

Tuttle did not show up. The Reverend Seely followed his barrel chest into the room, brows nettled, a big smile, hand stuck out before him. Keegan leaned across the desk and shook it. Seely's hair looked dyed. Well, that's show biz. Delphine he recognized, but not the other woman. She was Jo from the Gutter Ball.

"Tell the man, daughter," Seely said, turning to Jo. "I authorize you to tell this officer of the Law how God has sent down His wrath upon this sinful city."

Delphine said, "It's about Barbara Rooney and Angela Sykes. Jo knows who did it. She saw him in the Gutter Ball."

"I don't know his name." Josephine spoke in a quick nervous voice as if she were having doubts about doing this.

"It sounds like Martin Olson the dentist to me," Delphine said. "We showed her the newspaper picture."

"I'm not sure," Josephine piped.

Agnes took over then, getting the three of them settled and then asking for a clearer account of why they were here.

"To name a murderer, sister. This man may indeed be God's instrument but he is no less a sinner for that. He too shall have the divine wrath visited upon him."

Agnes nodded as if she could not agree more. To Josephine she said, "When I questioned you, you said you had nothing to say because you knew nothing."

"I know."

"You told Lieutenant Horvath little more."

"I didn't think I should. Those women, well, you know what they were doing, what everyone does at the Gutter Ball."

"You must sever relations with that den of iniquity at once," Seely thundered. Delphine looked nervous.

"I will," Josephine chirped. She turned to Agnes as if she could not bear the condemnation in Reverend Seely's eyes. "I saw this man both times. He followed the two women out the night Mrs. Rooney was killed and he was waiting in the back seat of the other woman's car in the parking lot. When I read that they had died, each time I knew what had happened. And I knew why."

"Why?" Keegan asked.

"God was punishing them." She looked at Seely and received an approving nod. She was back in his good graces.

"What picture did you show her?" Agnes asked Delphine.

"Dr. Martin Olson. We showed her several from the paper, about those deaths. Olson's was the one she picked."

Agnes looked at Keegan. "I called him a little while ago to tell him the ruling on Linger and Wippel. He is at his clinic."

One way, the wrong way, to do it would have been to take this whole menagerie over to Olson's clinic and have a big confrontation scene. In Keegan's experience, meetings meant to force an issue, squeeze a confession from a suspect, invariably misfired and left matters more complicated than they had been. On the other hand, it was difficult to know exactly what he was going to do or say at the clinic. What was clear was that he had to give Josephine a good look at Olson and if she said he was the one, make an arrest. To hell with Robertson. The chief refused to hear any reference made to the Rooney and Sykes deaths. For him the statute of limitations on those had run out several days ago. Keegan had hoped Francis Rooney would bring pressure on the department but when Barbara Rooney's husband employed Tuttle as counsel, Keegan was ready to give up himself. But if he really had been tempted to do that, Horvath and Agnes Lamb would have made it difficult. They had gone on pursuing the case oblivious to any difficulties Keegan might have with the chief over their activities. If Josephine pointed the finger at Olson, that was good enough for Keegan.

Agnes said, "Lieutenant Horvath could go pick him up."

Keegan considered her face and decided that her expression was not insolent. The fact was the suggestion was a good one. Cy could have Olson down here before the oral surgeon knew quite what was going on. If Josephine could not say he was the one, okay. They could talk to him about burying Wanda Wippel. "Go get him, Lamb." When Agnes had gone, Josephine and Tuttle's secretary went into a huddle in the corner of the office and the Reverend Seely paced up and down as if he were trying to determine the number of cubits that had been allotted to the captain of detectives. From time to time he paused and studied Keegan from beneath his bushy dyed brows. Phil Keegan frowned too as he flipped through reports and generally created the impression of a public servant hard at work.

"Hello, Reverend Seely," Cy said when he came into the room.

Seely nodded, pleased to be immediately recognized.

"Agnes tell you the story, Cy?"

Horvath nodded. "I'll go pick him up."

"Don't go into details with him."

"I'll just tell him we need his assistance. Agnes coming with me?"

"No! No, I want her to give me a hand here."

Keegan darted his eyes significantly, now at Reverend Seely, now at the two women. The slight alteration of the corners of Horvath's mouth might have been a smile. Keegan had half a mind to leave Horvath here and go for Olson himself, but before he could say anything Cy was out of the office.

32

IT WAS NEARLY four-thirty when Cy Horvath drove out of the police garage and headed toward Olson's clinic. Traffic was not yet heavy but he could not make the time he would have liked to.

As soon as Agnes told him Josephine's story, it rang true. He should have pressed his hunch that the bartender knew a lot more than she was telling. The Gutter Ball. That was the connection, but would he ever have thought of Olson? This kind of speculation was pointless. What mattered was that they were onto Olson at last.

What cars there were in the clinic parking lot were on the periphery. Employees? Horvath wheeled into a place by the entrance and got rapidly out of the car.

Inside, Horvath bounced across the indoor/outdoor carpeting to a counter behind which sat a nurse whose hair had the look of cotton candy except that it was ink black. Her eyeshadow had sparkling dust in it and when she looked up Horvath fully expected her to bat her false eyelashes at him.

"Dr. Olson," he said. "My name's Horvath."

She ran a Dragon Lady fingernail down the page of the book open before her.

Horvath said, "I don't have an appointment. It's about Miss Wippel. We need Dr. Olson's help. Is he in?"

The receptionist's mouth dropped open at the mention of Wippel and an unconvincing tragic look took possession of her features.

"He's in his office, I believe. The priest is with him."

"I know where it is."

"Wait, I'll call and tell him..."

But Horvath was already headed down the hall. The priest is with him? What the hell did the woman mean?

Before Horvath was a third of the way down the hall, Olson emerged from a doorway and without looking back went at a fast clip away from the detective.

"Doctor," Horvath called. "Just a minute."

Olson stopped and turned around so quickly he nearly lost his balance. The look on his face was one of pure terror.

"What are you doing here?" His voice came from his throat as water comes from a squeezed rag.

"Something has come up, Dr. Olson. Captain Keegan would appreciate it if you'd come downtown with me and help us out on something."

"Help you out? I'm already taking care of the funeral."

"I understand that. This is something different."

"I can't come now. Is it urgent?"

"Captain Keegan would like you to come immediately."

Olson shook his head violently. "No. No, I am to meet someone for dinner. Florence Day. We will discuss Miss Wippel's funeral."

"What priest is here?"

Olson's expression when he first saw Horvath was as nothing compared to the terror now in his eyes. He went into a half crouch, as if to protect himself.

"What priest?"

"Your receptionist said a priest is with you."

"She's lying! What would a priest be doing here?"

But Olson's eyes kept darting past Horvath, back in the direction they both had come. Horvath turned and looked at the doorway out of which Olson had come moments before. He started toward it and as he did, Olson jumped him. The dentist let out a cry and sprang and landed on Horvath's back. Cy just kept going and Olson clung to him, riding piggyback to the open doorway. Horvath could see the body in the dentist's chair by the light from the hallway but it was only when he turned the room light on that he saw it was Roger Dowling.

At the sight of the priest, Horvath shook Olson off and the dentist hit the floor with a despairing shout that was very nearly drowned out by the scream of the receptionist. By the time Horvath was leaning over the dentist's chair, half the personnel of the clinic was converging on the scene.

Roger Dowling's eyes fluttered and opened and he looked at Horvath in a dazed fashion. His right arm lifted from the armrest and rose eerily to fall upon his other.

"Shot," the priest managed to say, and then his eyes closed and a smile spread across his thin lips.

At first Horvath did not understand. Olson did not permit him the leisure to ponder the priest's remark. Picking himself up from the floor, he hurled himself once more at Horvath. Cy brushed him aside and Olson spun past the chair. And then he lunged again, this time for a hypodermic on the round table connected with the chair. A scream from the hallway accompanied this attempt. Horvath had had enough of Olson. He drove his fist into the dentist's face. The blow sent him reeling backward. He hit the wall and then slid limply into a sitting position, as out as Roger

Dowling. A nurse came in and retrieved the hypodermic needle.

"What is that?" Horvath asked.

"Probably sodium pentathol."

"Is it harmful?"

"Harmful?" She smiled, then grew stern. "Far from it. Most people find it very enjoyable."

Roger Dowling seemed to be among them. He began to mumble and then burst out laughing. The nurse smiled again and did not try to wipe it away.

"That's normal. People just babble away under that stuff."

"Watch him, will you? I have to make a phone call."

He shooed the rest of them away and went down the hall to the receptionist's desk. When he picked up the phone to call Keegan he felt better than he had in weeks.

33

It was a sunny Sunday afternoon and Phil Keegan and Roger Dowling, come from the brunch Mrs. Murkin had waiting for them when they returned from the noon Mass, settled before the television in the study. Phil fiddled with the dials, trying to bring the picture from Soldiers' Field into better focus. It was that moment just before kick-off when it is still possible to hope the Bears will win. Mrs. Murkin, in the doorway, looked with frowning approval on these preparations.

"I suppose you'll want popcorn."

"At half time," Phil Keegan said, still fine-tuning.

Marie Murkin nodded, waiting for Captain Keegan to be seated. When he was, she put her hands on her hips.

"Has Dr. Olson confessed to all those killings?"

Phil, with one eye on the set, nodded impatiently. "He can't give us enough details. Loves to go on about it."

"And to think he was my dentist!" The housekeeper's eyes rounded in speculative horror.

"What kind of anesthetic did he use on you, Marie?" Roger Dowling asked, tamping tobacco into his pipe.

"I don't know."

"How long were you out?"

"I don't know. Why?"

"No reason."

She didn't believe him. It was a confessable fault, this teasing of Marie Murkin. She seemed to be running her tongue around inside her mouth.

"I have half a mind to have the work he did on me done over."

"He pull a tooth or what?" Phil touched a match to his cigar and began to puff blue-gray smoke into the study.

Marie's chin tilted upward and her brows arched. She clearly had no intention of going into detail on her dental surgery with Phil Keegan. Perhaps she thought the extensive repairs suggested an age older than hers. "I'll take forty winks before making the popcorn."

"I guess it's pretty serious when you go to a guy like Olson. I mean, he didn't just do fillings."

The drift of the conversation sent Marie Murkin down the hall. Access to her room was from the kitchen. Phil settled back contentedly and glared at the set. The Bears' coaching staff was being scanned by the camera and memories of past humiliations dimmed Phil Keegan's anticipatory pleasure.

"I wonder if he would have killed me, Phil?"

"Yup."

"You sound pretty sure."

"I am. Olson said that was what he was going to do."

"Then Cy saved my life."

"I sent him out there."

Roger Dowling nodded. "If I was in real danger, it spoils a little theory of mine. I felt no fear. I have always believed that when death is really imminent, I will know it and be afraid."

"It wasn't a good test, Roger. He had you on Cloud Nine with sodium pentathol. You were babbling like a brook when I got there."

"Edifying babble, I hope."

"Couldn't make it out. Sounded like a sermon."

This ambiguity lay upon the air with their tobacco smoke. It was difficult to tell if Phil had intended it.

"Reverend Seely has invited me to be a guest preacher in his pulpit."

"You going to do it?"

"It's the least I can do."

"How so?"

"He claims he saved my life."

Keegan considered that with half-closed eyes. He seemed to consider and then reject various remarks. The kick-off relieved him of the need to say anything. He angled his shoulders back toward the screen.

Roger Dowling followed only fitfully the televised game, which was punctuated by Phil's groans. He thought of those Martin Olson had killed, a senseless series of murders that might have extended to include his own. Mrs. Rooney, Angela Sykes, Georgie, and Wanda Wippel. Florence Day would have been next if he had not gone to the clinic. How adroitly Olson had overpowered him and shot the sodium pentathol into him. The euphoria he had felt might have encompassed his death. That continued to horrify him. Death is horrible and should always seem so, particularly when it comes to take us. And now it would come for Martin Olson.

He must go see the oral surgeon. He would complete the intention that had taken him to the clinic. Now that Olson's punishment was assured, he was that much readier for mercy. Not human forgiveness — who could extend that to a man who had murdered four fellow human beings? But there is One who is the union of justice and mercy and it was before His bar that he hoped to bring Martin Olson.

Phil Keegan groaned from his cloud of cigar smoke. The Bears disgraced themselves. But the sun shone. It was hard to believe that winter was near.

"The defense isn't bad," Phil Keegan said. His voice was that of a man in desperate search of a bright note. Roger nodded and concentrated on the game.